Traffic

A Ronnie Lake Murder Mystery

Niki Danforth

By

Niki Danforth

Publisher: Pancora Press
Book Design: www.polgarusstudio.com
Cover Art: Colin Durrant at Prime Designs

As always, for Dan

PROLOGUE

Marissa Popov stared up at the pointed tip of the soaring steel and glass tower as she and Natalia waited for the light to change. The way it pierced the sky into the fog made her feel as if she could shoot to the moon from the spear-like top of the building.

The tugging on her coat sleeve shifted her gaze back to her ten-year-old sister.

"When I go to college one day, I don't want a backpack anymore." Natalia moved one of her pack's shoulder straps and leaned in against her older sibling as they waited for the light. She played with the strap on Marissa's small cross-body woven leather bag. "If you get tired of this one, may I borrow it?"

"Probably." Marissa had forgotten Natalia's inhaler, and they were backtracking to pick it up before heading to school. She looked up again at the high floors of the building.

"You always look up there." Natalia nudged Marissa. "How come? Do you think Pappa can see us? You know, when he's home."

She laughed. "No, I don't think he can see us from way up there."

"When will he come home?" Worry washed over the girl's face, and she scrutinized the sidewalk under her feet.

"I think tomorrow." The light changed and they held hands." She gave Natalia's a squeeze.

The two dashed across Central Park South, the younger girl's ginger ponytail flying out behind her and the choppy strands of her older sister's honey-blonde hair whipping in the chilly November wind. They moved quickly along the sidewalk, Marissa looking ahead to maneuver through the crowd. The girls darted left and right to pass slower pedestrians as they made their way to the tower.

"You won't leave me?" Natalia pulled on her sister's hand.

This was a drill that Natalia and Marissa had repeated many times in the last year, ever since the child's mother had died. Marissa remembered her own broken heart when her mother died twelve years earlier. Her father had remarried quickly. Then along came Natalia, her adorable half-sister.

"We'll stay safe until he comes home?" the girl asked, her voice quivering. Marissa leaned down to give her a hug.

As they swept through the enormous tinted glass doors, Marissa reassured Natalia that all was good. How could they not stay safe—the security in this tower was like Fort Knox, even though most of the residents had not yet moved into their apartments and there was still a lot of construction going on inside the building. Three doormen, two deskmen, and sentries by each elevator greeted, waved, and high-fived the kid as if she were one of their own. Natalia loved to high-five them right back.

The sisters swallowed to clear their ears as they exited the private super-express elevator to the forty-second floor. Marissa opened her bag for the key and unlocked the door. They walked into the foyer of the spacious, luxe apartment owned by their father, Maxim Popov.

Marissa came face-to-face with a painting that she, a college art history major, never tired of admiring and studying—one of the forest paintings by the Russian avant-garde painter Natalia Goncharova from the early twentieth century. It had been her father's wedding gift to the last Mrs. Popov, and she'd named her daughter after the artist. The other walls of the foyer displayed additional turn-of-the-century canvasses, further evidence that her Moldovan father's passion for Russian art knew no limits. Marissa never took for granted living among these great paintings. She picked up the inhaler from the round marble table in the middle of the foyer.

Natalia dropped her pack on the floor, opened it, and dug around inside. Some of her school things spilled out, but she focused on her sister. "Red Bull, please, please, please." She pulled on Marissa's arm. "I'm getting one."

"Okay, okay, Talia! But quickly." She allowed Natalia to drag her along as the two of them headed to the kitchen.

Right before the door, she glanced up at the last moment and saw that one of the tiny cameras in the corner near the ceiling looked smashed.

Momentum carried them forward through the door, and it was too late to stop. Marissa noted a figure in her peripheral vision. Before she could grab Natalia and run, three other men out of nowhere joined the first one, all with faces hidden by sunglasses and fleece neck gators, ball caps, or hoodies.

Everything stopped for a split-second and then chaos broke out. One of the men stumbled and knocked into the others. They recovered swiftly and rushed toward the girls, yelling at each other in a jumble of Spanish.

"What do we do?" a younger-sounding one shrieked in panic in accented English. He grabbed Natalia and she screamed. The first man, stocky and strong, bellowed a response in a commanding, gruff voice.

Marissa swung her bag at one of the other intruders and simultaneously lunged forward to protect her sister. But a tall man grabbed her shoulders from behind and pulled her off her feet. She twisted as she fell and her face slammed against the kitchen island, her nose taking the full impact.

"Unhhh," she exhaled.

"Marissa!" Natalia howled.

Marissa's arm slapped back against the island surface, trying to grab something, anything, as a weapon. All she could come up with was a glass. It slipped from her hand and crashed onto the floor, breaking into pieces. She cried out as she fell on top of the shards.

"Owww," she moaned, and the man lifted her roughly into a standing position. She noticed blood dripping from her nose, which hurt like hell, and it was difficult to breathe.

The man shoved her forward, and she pulled away as hard as she could, emitting a loud grunt. She broke free to reach for her sister, but he grabbed her forcefully.

"Marissa!" Natalia cried out again as three of the men dragged them fighting and screaming through a butler's pantry. Natalia tried to hang onto the handle of the small refrigerator and Marissa grabbed at the dishwasher door, hoping for a weapon but seeing only the blood spatter left by her nosebleed.

She slowed her breathing, attempting to calm herself for her sister's sake. Natalia was gasping and crying as they stumbled into the dining room.

"I'm right here with you, Talia." Marissa's sister gradually quieted down.

The men yelled back and forth and pushed the girls into chairs next to each other. One of the men pulled his shoelaces from his sneakers, threw one to his buddy, and they clumsily bound the girls' wrists tightly to the leg of the dining table.

"Ow, it hurts!" Natalia started to cry again, kicking her foot several times against the leg of the table in protest.

"Hey, take it easy. You're scaring her." Marissa's heart pounded wildly, and she tried to act calm. "What do you want?"

The stocky man came into the room and registered surprise and anger at the sight of the sisters tied to the table. He pulled at the shoestrings binding their wrists and looked around the room, complaining in Spanish. He spotted a bundle of cables near a baseboard, pointed at the zip tie keeping the bundle together, and sent the young man back to the kitchen.

An older man, from the sound of his scratchy voice, pulled out his reading glasses and rushed over to a sideboard to examine a photograph of a middle-aged man with the two sisters. "Maxim…" He switched the glasses back to his shades, turned to look at the girls, and started to say something else.

Marissa jumped in. "You don't need to tie us up—"

"Shut up, lady," the older man said in heavily accented English, trying to sound tough. Even with his sandpaper voice, something was off. "You talk too much—"

Natalia let loose a high-pitched cry like a mortally wounded animal. It turned into body-wracking sobs that made it hard for her to breathe. Marissa could see signs of an asthma attack coming on.

"Keep your eyes closed, Talia. It will be less scary,"

she said in a gentle tone, but her sister still sobbed loudly.

The stocky man, growled something authoritatively in Spanish and left the room again.

Two other guys followed him. That left the tall one. Natalia's crying showed no sign of subsiding.

"Please," Marissa pleaded. "Let me help my sister. I may have dropped her inhaler in the kitchen." She mimicked sneezing and using an inhaler. "Do you understand? You don't want her to pass out, especially if your boss plans to call our father. I'm guessing that's why you're here. You want something from him?"

"Shut up. Not your business," he barked at her, his accent Latino, too.

Marissa called out as he left the room, "And please some ice and a towel for my nose."

"I'm scared." Natalia's voice broke and the tears flowed harder.

"Take long, deep breaths," she said in a quiet voice, hoping to calm her sister. Natalia still squeezed her eyes shut. Marissa worked on loosening her bound wrists.

A few minutes later, the tall man returned with a toolbox and a small metal bowl. He walked into the dining room just in time to catch Marissa trying to free herself.

"Stop," he ordered. He opened the toolbox and pulled out a couple of zip ties. Natalia continued crying.

"Keep her quiet." He untied the shoestring around Marissa's wrists as she spoke to her sister in a soothing tone. He zip-tied one of her wrists to the leg of the table.

He then repeated the same process with Natalia and one of her wrists.

He reached into the toolbox and handed Marissa the inhaler. He checked one more time that the tie to her other arm was tight and did the same with Natalia. Then he handed Marissa a kitchen towel and the bowl, which she saw was filled with ice.

"Manuel," a man called from further down the hallway.

"Thank you, Manuel," Marissa said as he left.

She helped Natalia with the inhaler, whispering, "It'll all be okay. Breathe slowly. We will figure out a way."

After a couple of puffs on the inhaler, Natalia's eyes popped open. She took one look at her older sister's bloody nose and sobbed even harder. Marissa rubbed Natalia's back. Eventually the girl's breathing slowed down, and her crying turned into whimpering. Marissa wrapped a handful of ice cubes in the towel and, leaning forward, pressed the cubes against her nose.

She could hear the men arguing. "Shhh, Talia. I need to listen," she said, her tone still soothing, even though she wanted to throw up she was so scared.

She couldn't make out what they were saying except for a word here and there. "…Popov…"

"…police…"

Marissa put the ice cubes to the side and slid her free hand into her short leather boot until she felt her phone tucked below her ankle. She pulled it out and lifted it, and the device slipped from her hand. She tried to catch it, but ended up accidentally swatting away the phone as it fell to the ground.

With one arm still zip-tied to the leg of the table, she stretched. The fingertips of her free arm touched the edge of the phone, but not enough to grab it. Marissa scrambled to reach farther in order to retrieve her phone.

She paused for a moment, took a few deep breaths, and tried not to panic.

~~~~~

Samantha James was the most eye-catching bike messenger anyone in the paved canyons of Manhattan could ever have hoped to see. Her long red hair flew out from beneath her helmet and her ultra-long legs pumped the pedals while she darted between stop-and-go traffic. Often vehicles around her would slow down trying to get a better look as she raced by, clad in her brightly-patterned leggings. Samantha was definitely attention-grabbing, as she deftly negotiated traffic behind the aviator shades that sat on her upturned, slightly crooked nose. Every now and then a cabbie would whistle in appreciation of her bike-handling skills, and she'd respond with her quirky, gap-toothed smile.

Unfortunately, casting directors hadn't been swayed by her unconventional looks and acting talent lately. As she cruised down Fifth Avenue to deliver a package—signed legal papers to an address in the Hudson Yards area—she thought about the audition from the day before. She was sure she'd nailed the part of the rebellious law student. Ben, who was doing the casting, liked her work, and she knew the director, Jerzy White, socially. She'd even had a small semi-regular part on one of his cop shows a year ago, so they knew she was a pro. But there wasn't even a lousy call-back on her phone for this new one.

As she flew around a corner on 38th Street, a taxi almost doored her as the passenger stepped out on the traffic side of the cab. She'd seen it swing open at the very last minute.

"Hey! Watch out!" Samantha cried out. She'd just managed to swerve away and avoid slamming into the yellow door.

"No, YOU watch out," a woman yelled from the sidewalk. "Crazy jerk!"

"Always weaving in and out of traffic," another woman complained. "You're gonna cause an accident, you hear me?"

Samantha ignored the angry women and felt fortunate to have this new part-time messenger gig since she'd quit her old job to go back to school. She slowed down for an upcoming pedestrian crossing and stopped.

"Hey, babe, where ya goin'?" a younger guy yelled out from a group in the middle of the crossing. His chortling friends fake-slugged him.

Samantha pushed off and ignored them as she pedaled by.

"Bitch!" the guy yelled after her.

CHAPTER ONE

-Appointment at 11:30 cancelled. Can I
take my lovely daughter to lunch at noon?

-Sorry, Mom. Got a deadline. Maybe later.

-OK. Next time. Are you

My phone rang and my fingers stopped texting. I clicked connect. "Hi, Brooke."

"Hi Mom. What are you doing in the city this early? Where are you?"

"Hudson Yards. I just finished an appointment with a silver dealer. It was the only time he could see me today—"

"A silver dealer? What's going on?"

"I brought a couple of things of your great-grandmother's and photos of the rest of what I might like to sell. Remember, we talked about this the last time you were at the house?"

"Oh, Mom, you've been in major clean-out mode." Brooke laughed. Even through the phone, it was always music to my ears.

"Honey, I'm asking you again, are you sure you don't want any of this family silver? If you do, I won't sell the pieces you'd like to have. You know, for one day when you get married and have a family of your own?" Then I quickly added, "Some of them are from Tiffany's way, way, way back in the day."

"Mom, when the time comes, I plan to register at IKEA, not Tiffany's. What about Jess?"

"Your sister pretty much told me the same thing." I thought back to Jess's choice of Amazon, when I'd last spoken with her. "It's fine. I'll sell them and donate the money to charity."

"I know what that means—our local animal shelter. Sounds like a good plan," Brooke said. "So, who's looking after Warrior while you're in town?"

"Your aunt, Juliana, which is lucky for me." My sister-in-law had a strong connection with my beloved German Shepherd, and almost always volunteered to babysit.

"Lucky for Warrior," my daughter said. "What's next on your agenda?"

"You know me. I come in for one thing and then I add on as the day progresses. Thought I'd see the fun new exhibit at the Costume Institute at the Met and then had hoped coffee with an old friend—"

"Ooooh, Mom. Is that old friend a 'man'?" Brooke giggled through the phone. "And is he really 'old'? Like sixty-plus? If he is, you'll leave him in the dust."

I laughed. "Hold it, young lady. I was meeting a

friend from college, but it was cancelled—"

"Tell me one thing. Are you dressed like one of those ladies-who-lunch, or do you have on a cool-mom-outfit?"

I glance down at my honey-colored, classic Burberry trench coat, my black wool trousers, and my honey and black plaid Diane B flats with the shiny black buckle, shoes that I'd only ever buy during big-time sales. "Well, I'd like to think cool mom with a *little* bit ladies-who-lunch."

"Mom, gotta run," Brooke interrupted. "My boss is waving at me. I'll text if things change with lunch. Love ya!"

"Love you, too—" *Click.* "—Brooke?" But she was already gone.

Just my luck—an available New York taxi was close by on Ninth Avenue and driving in my direction. I flagged him down, opened the back door, and slid my tote bag onto the seat. As I climbed into the cab, my foot stepped onto something bulky, almost causing me to lose my balance. I bounced onto the seat with a grunt and pulled the door shut.

"I'm heading up town," I said, giving him the address. "How's traffic this morning?"

The taxi's radio crackled over the driver's gravelly voice. "Not bad, but the President's here for the UN and a lot of streets are closed off." He stopped for the light.

"Oh, great." I looked at the driver's profile on the screen inside the cab and quickly typed his code into my app.

I gently kicked at the lump that had almost caused me to trip getting in. It was soft. "What's this?" I tapped it again with my foot.

"What's going on back there?" the cabbie asked.

"There's something on the floor."

"No way. I cleaned it before I started my shift."

I looked down at the lump more closely. "Unbelievable." My hand brushed across the famous Louis Vuitton logo design on the pebbled leather of a large duffle bag. "Oh my god. Is this real?"

"Hey," he barked.

I glanced into the rearview mirror to meet his eyes. "There's a large duffle bag on the floor."

"Must've been my last fare."

"Where'd you drop him?"

"Them. A couple. They were in a rush. At the airport. Then I went on break to eat something." He looked at me with more interest.

"Which airport?"

"LaGuardia."

I unzipped the duffle and saw an orange Hermès gift box and a soft, stuffed child's lambie on top. I rooted around the bag to see what else was in there. "There's a wallet," I said more to myself. "Maybe I can find a name."

"Huh, what'd you say?" he growled.

I didn't say anything as I continued looking through the bag, and the driver glanced back at me. The light turned green, but the bumper-to-bumper traffic moved agonizingly slow.

"You can't go through someone's bag in my cab. Hand it over." His voice was getting snarky and there was determination in his tone.

It looked like a real Louis Vuitton bag and they cost a lot of money. "Hmm, I don't know..." I quickly zipped it up.

The driver's head glanced back again, trying to see the bag. He swerved to avoid a pedestrian.

I grabbed the side door handle to not get thrown to the other side of the backseat. "That was close."

He reached his arm through the open partition of the cab, waving his hand in the air in a 'gimme' fashion. "Here, I'll take it."

"Whoa." I held onto it tightly. "What do you plan to do with it? Maybe with the wallet, I can get it back to the owner."

"My cab, my bag, my wallet." His tone had shifted from gravelly to greedy.

"I'd like to track down the owners—"

"Listen, it's their loss and I'm not asking again—" The driver grabbed his steering wheel at the last moment to swerve out of the way of a Toyota that had cut in front without a turn signal.

"Watch out!" I screamed, quickly shifting my tote and the mystery bag as close as possible as I scooted near the door.

Then he hit the brakes and the Toyota screeched to a halt at the red light at the next intersection. I threw open the door a moment before he hit the lock button to make me a hostage. I clumsily jumped out, dragging the Louis Vuitton bag behind me. The driver almost lurched through the partition reaching for the duffle, but he could only grab one corner. I twisted my body away from the cab, and the bag's corner slipped from his hand.

"Damn, you f—ing bitch. That's mine." He jumped out of his cab in the standstill traffic at the red light, screaming at me, "Bring it back, bitch. I've got you on the app paying for the ride. I'll find you. You'll wish you'd never f—ed with me."

I stood on the sidewalk, people dashing in all directions around me. I rushed down a side street jammed with cars and trucks. Darting between a van and a truck that blocked me from the cab driver, I hurried into the first door I came to. My own tote and the mystery satchel banged against the door's glass panes as I stumbled into the lobby of an office building. I moved to the side and watched for the out-of-control driver through the dark tinted window.

He stood by his cab, yelling. I could see him, but he couldn't see me.

The light turned green and drivers blasted their horns for him to get moving. Resigned and muttering under his breath—probably profanities—he jumped back into his cab.

I waited until I saw another fare get in and he drove away. *No way was that driver planning to take this bag to lost-and-found. I'll find the owner,* I thought to myself.

Once again, I clunked through the door with my bag and the duffle, still staring in the direction of the departing taxi and not looking where I was walking. I tripped on the sidewalk, and the motion sent me flying forward off the curb and into the street, dropping the bags around me, but fortunately I didn't fall. I leaned over to pick up my belongings and heard a skidding noise behind me, as well as another string of profanities.

I turned just in time to see a young woman on a bicycle barreling down on me, shouting, "Holy shit, lady. Out of my way!"

She bounced her bike onto the sidewalk to avoid hitting me on her right and a car on her left. She whipped to the side to stop herself, but it was too late. "Watch where you're going!" she cried out, skidding at an angle down the sidewalk. Other people jumped out of the way, yelling at her.

Even though she handled the bicycle expertly and avoided hitting me, the woman crashed to the ground, moaning, "F— me. Owwww."

She still straddled the bike even when she stopped sliding. As she carefully checked her limbs and adjusted her helmet and messenger bag, I could see that her leg and forearm closest to the sidewalk were pretty scraped up.

Pulling my bags with me from the street, I scrambled to her aid. "Are you okay? I'm sorry, I stepped right in front of you. It's my fault." I noticed the scrapes were bleeding. "Can I help you? Let me call 911." I pulled my phone out of my pocket.

"No! Do *not* call 911!" she said. "I'm fine." Still on the ground, she examined her bike.

Her phone buzzed as I leaned over to assist her, and she pulled it out of her sports bra inside her vest and fleece jacket. As she checked the message, her face went ashen and her body stiffened as if she'd received an electric shock. I pulled back fast.

"Oh my god, Marissa," she said under her breath, staring at the screen.

The young woman looked up at me, her eyes shifting from anger to shock to extreme fear in all of a second. Likewise, her body tensed while she quickly scanned the people passing by. It was as if she were readying herself for fight or flight.

"Are you alright?" I asked. "Is everything okay?"

She pushed up and shook me off as I tried to help her. "Besides you causing an accident, you mean?"

"Hey, there's a good reason why I wasn't paying attention," I protested. "Of course, I'll pay for any damage to your bicycle."

"Yeah, yeah, yeah." She continued checking her bike and glancing around nervously.

"Are you expecting someone?"

She looked at me as if she didn't know what I was talking about.

"You're looking around as if you're watching for someone."

"No. I'm fine."

Her response was too speedy. I took a deep breath and tried to slow things down. "You got a message that upset you. Are you sure you're okay?"

Her jaw clenched, and she stared icily at me, not revealing anything. As we appraised each other, I made a snap decision.

"I can help."

"With what? My bike?" She rolled her eyes as she pushed it back and forth. "I think it's okay." She was still jittery as she got on it, ready to pedal away.

"No, with whatever bad news you got." Thinking of my daughters, who were not much older than this young woman, I was concerned.

"You? You're kidding. You look like one of those rich ladies who go to lunch all the time," she said, sneering. "I don't have time for this." She rolled her bicycle to the edge of the sidewalk.

"You received some kind of shocking news about Marissa—"

"How do you know her name?" she snapped, whipping her head back so fast her long red hair almost hit me in the face.

"You said it when you got the message, and you reacted as if it was really bad news." I fished around my bag, pulled out a business card, and gave it to her. "Here, take it."

She did take it and glanced at it. She looked at it again and then at me. "*You're* a private eye? For real?

No way."

"Yes, a licensed private investigator."

The young woman tucked it in her back pocket then pushed her bike off the curb and onto the street.

"If it's really serious, you should go to the police," I urged. "But if you feel you can't, I can help. And I know other people who can help, too."

"Right." She rolled her eyes again before giving me a dismissive wave and pedaling off, merging into traffic.

CHAPTER TWO

I needed a moment to catch my breath. I could still see the upset expression on the bike messenger's face when she got the text. *Well, she's got my number if she needs help*, I thought to myself.

I paid for my tea at a nearby coffee shop and leaned against a counter by the window. It was time to take a closer look at the Louis Vuitton duffle bag, so I plopped it on the counter next to my coffee.

First, I noticed the bag was well-worn and supple, as if used a lot. I unzipped the duffle and pulled the dark brown handles apart to look inside. There on top sat an iconic, flat, tangerine-colored Hermès box tied with brown ribbon. A stuffed animal, a soft lamb, sat wedged against one corner of the box. I carefully lifted out the cardboard container, as if its contents had come from a bank vault. The larger size of the square box made it perfect for holding more than a beautiful silk scarf, perhaps a silk shawl instead. I resisted my nosy urge to untie the ribbon…for the moment anyway, until I learned more.

I set the package on the table and reached into the bag for the animal. I looked face-to-face at an adorable white lamb. It was super-soft and very cuddly with a frayed off-white ribbon tied in a bow around its neck. The lamb looked even more worn out than the Louis Vuitton duffle, so the bag's owner was probably a parent or grandparent. Today's copy of *The Wall Street Journal* sat on top of a pair of large dark brown leather gloves, which pointed to a man as the possible owner of this bag.

At the bottom, I saw the brown leather wallet I'd first glimpsed in the taxi. I flipped it open, hoping to find a driver's license, credit card, or some other ID that would help me locate the owner. I struck out. While the wallet contained a lot of cash, there was nothing else in it, not even a photo of a loved one. Whoever owned this bag probably carried credit cards and a license in his pockets, just in case he got separated from the duffle. I decided to start with the scarf.

The Hermès store wasn't too far away, just over on Madison Avenue. Inside was a brightly-colored, elegant interior of silk scarves and shawls and a rainbow display of men's silk ties. I feasted my eyes on their gorgeous leather bags, even though they were way beyond my budget.

A young sales woman asked if she could help me, and I told her about the bag and the box inside.

"I haven't opened it yet, so I don't know what kind of scarf the owner of this bag bought." I placed it on a table.

"The box is a bit larger than the ones for scarves. Let's open it and see what it is. I can retie the ribbon for you." Her dark pixie haircut reminded me of a young Audrey Hepburn. I couldn't help but admire the top she'd created by tying together two red, white, and blue silk scarves of giraffes and belting them with a third, creating a kind of soft vest over a white knit turtleneck top. Her look was stunning.

She pulled out a silk shawl larger than the scarves she was wearing. Shaking it out, she held it up for me to see, revealing a glorious design of a sleeping jaguar with a magnificent headdress of blue feathers.

"This is beautiful," I said, taking it from her. "Do you remember selling this scarf in the last several days, maybe to a man who carried a duffle like this one? I realize it's a long shot, but I want to return the bag to him."

"I can check to see how many we've sold in the last week, but I wouldn't guess many. The shawls are more expensive than the scarves. I'll be back in a moment." She walked around the corner of a display and disappeared.

Five minutes later as I was refolding the shawl, the sales woman returned with a big smile. "I was right. We've only sold two of these in the last several weeks at this store. And I spoke to my colleague who remembers selling one of them two days ago."

"You're kidding." I couldn't believe my good luck.

"She told me she remembered the sale because the couple bought it for his mother, who loves jaguars. She remembered that he said it was his mother's favorite cat."

"Can you please contact them and ask if the scarf was lost?" I asked. "If they say yes, please ask them to call me as soon as possible." I handed her my card.

She read it and looked up at me in bewilderment and blurted, "You're a private investigator? I'm sorry, but you don't look like any private eye I've ever seen on TV or in the movies," she responded sheepishly.

"You're the second person who's told me that this morning. Thank you for your help, uh—"

"Chloe." She smiled.

"Thanks, Chloe." I smiled back as I headed for the door with the duffle and my tote.

"Wait, wait!" she called after me. "You dropped this." She waved the toy lamb at me.

"Oh my god. Thank you." I took the stuffed animal from her and looked at the toy. "It looks so well-loved that I'd hate to lose this and have somebody's child upset with me. Besides our lead on the shawl, I wish this little lamb could help me find the owner, too."

Chloe's face lit up. "Why don't you post a picture on Facebook? Do you have an account?"

"Well, yes, but I hardly use it."

She took the lamb back and propped it carefully on the arm of an upholstered chair so that it looked even more adorable. "Okay, snap a couple of cute pictures and pick your favorite," she instructed, which I did.

As I set up the post, I commented, "Do you really

think this could work? I only use it with my daughters, so I don't have a lot of activity in my account."

"Here, tag me," Chloe said. "I've got a lot of nice people who see my Facebook and Instagram because I post a lot of photos for the store. You know, like creative ways to wear the scarves."

"Sounds great." It was a long shot, but I posted the toy to my Facebook with a message.

One sad lambie looking for its family. If your child's or grandchild's lamb is lost, PM me and tell me what kind of a bag you're missing, as well as what else is in the bag. Lambie wants to come home.

CHAPTER THREE

I wanted to go home, too, after my crazy morning. I picked up my car at the garage and began driving toward the West Side Highway. My phone dinged as I sat at a red light and I saw a text from someone named Samantha.

-Are you for real?

I responded with a voice text in my car.

-Who is this?

-I was on my bike on 9th Ave and you got in my way.

I pulled over on a side street to tap out a response.

-Nice to meet you, Samantha.

-Are you a real PI? You said call if I need help.

-Yes, I'm a licensed PI, and I can help.

-Meet me by the water fountain where you go into the park at Columbus Circle.

-See you soon.

Backtracking a few blocks, I pulled into a garage on Central Park South. I told the attendant I'd only be an hour and pleaded with him please keep the car close by.

I made my way along Central Park South and headed to Columbus Circle, still hauling my own tote and the mystery duffle bag that I wasn't letting out of my sight. I walked toward the spacious Merchant's Gate entrance at the park's southwest corner.

As usual, pedestrians, bicyclists, roller skaters, and kiosks of every sort filled the plaza surrounding the imposing Maine Monument. Even so, I spotted Samantha right away. She stood with her bicycle next to the fountain at the base of the statue. I walked toward her, waved, and caught her eye.

The expression on her face was one of disdain, even though she was the one who had called me. The corners of her mouth were slightly turned down and her eyes bore into mine.

I stopped, and she extended her hand tentatively.

"Hi, I'm Ronnie Lake." We shook. "And you?"

"Samantha James."

"Good to meet you, Samantha James." I sat down on the steps, indicating she should do the same. "Tell me what you—"

She cut me off. "Call me Sam." She reluctantly sat

down, keeping her bicycle close. "I want to hire you to help me get something that's mine."

"What is it and why can't you get it yourself?" I asked.

"Because I live across the street in the tower."

I followed Sam's gaze to a half-dozen skinny towers that almost disappeared into the foggy sky. I also took another look at her bike messenger clothes—the multi-colored leggings, the fleece, the vest, the helmet.

"You live in one of those?" I tried not to sound amazed, because I didn't know what I might be getting myself into. I'd felt responsible for her accident earlier, and I'd come out of guilt to help her.

"See the shorter one a block south of the park?" She tapped her foot nervously.

"Shorter is a relative term, isn't it," I remarked. "Shorter than the new towers around it, but taller than the buildings that have already been there for a while." I pointed at a grey glass tower that could have been sixty stories tall. It started wide and got progressively narrower with curved setbacks as the stories climbed higher. "How about the one that looks like a silver waterfall? That's where you live?"

"No, the one next to it." She pointed at another steel and glass tower, this one with a tip that reached into the cloudy sky. "On the forty-second floor." She sounded in a hurry and jumped up. "Come on. I'll fill you in." She grabbed her bike and pushed it as we walked.

While we waited for the light to change, I stared up

at her building, one among a handful of other new construction.

"How many apartments do you think are in there?" Sam nodded at her skyscraper.

"Oh…" I eyeballed the entire building. "A hundred, two hundred?"

She snorted with a cynical laugh. "Try forty."

"Only forty? But it looks like it has about sixty floors." I started counting. "Two, four, six, eight, ten, twelve—"

"The top sixteen floors are two-story apartments," she interrupted. "Other apartments take up an entire floor, or there are two to a floor."

We walked south toward 58th Street, and Sam continued talking. "If it were nighttime and you looked up there, you'd only see lights on in five or six of the units. The rest would be dark."

That piece of information did surprise me. "Where's everybody else? The other tenants?"

"Probably in some other country, or on their private jets flying to some other country."

"There aren't any full-time city residents living there?" I remembered reading about these towers in the papers a while back.

"These are the top one-percent of the one-percent," Sam said as we made a swift left turn down a narrow alley, "and they're mostly from other countries."

"How is it that you live up there?" I asked. "That's ridiculously expensive real estate."

She looked at me appraisingly. "Look, just because

I'm dressed to ride my bike, doesn't mean I'm not good enough to live there. My father and I are having a huge fight, and he's kicked me out, even though I've got my own key." She pulled a key out of her pocket and showed it to me.

"What do you mean, kicked you out?" I look at her skeptically.

"He told all the doormen not to let me in. Look, I'll pay you. Can you help me or not?" She was getting worked up and I noticed her breathing quickened.

"Ah, I don't know…what exactly is it you need from the apartment?"

"All my IDs are there, you know, birth certificate, Social Security card. I keep them in a safe place, and I need them." Her jaw clenched and her voice rose an octave.

This didn't add up, but I decided to play along to try find out more about Sam.

"And how am I supposed to get in?" I asked. "I can't just waltz in past the doorman. Security's tight in these buildings."

The tension in Sam's clenched jaw had rapidly moved to her neck muscles.

"Hey, slow down and take a deep breath," I said.

Sam paused for a second then launched back in.

"There's still a lot of construction going on inside the building on the different apartments. We'll start around the back, and you go in and pretend you're part of the design team for the apartment on the thirty-ninth floor. Tell them you're from Courtland Interiors, and say you're late for a meeting. Once you get there in the elevator, get off and take the stairs to the forty-second floor to my place." Sam gave me instructions on where to find her bedroom. "Look in my closet. You'll see a couple of shelves with sweaters. Check the bottom one. You should find an old navy blue messenger bag hidden behind the sweaters. Grab it. That's where I keep my papers."

She hurried me around another corner, all the while maneuvering her bicycle on and off the curbs.

"Where are we going?" I asked as we cut toward the back of the buildings.

"We're scoping out the perimeter. I want to show you the lay of the land."

We're scoping out the perimeter? After weaving among several other buildings, we stopped near a wide driveway in the back of Sam's building. It opened into a large courtyard. Several big trucks with construction materials were parked over on one side.

"This looks nice enough to be the front entrance of most Manhattan buildings," I remarked. I looked around for cameras and saw a couple that were placed strategically to cover the back. "But what's with all the trucks?"

"Like I said, a lot of construction crews are finishing different apartments before their owners arrive. And the fancy door isn't just the service entrance, it's also the valet parking. See that grey door in the building next to this one? Over to the right?"

I nodded. "Yeah?"

"That's a secret exit for the residents of my tower."

"You're kidding. In a different building?"

"Hey, that's how they built it. It's an escape route in case anybody tries to take over our building. It's top secret," she insisted.

I wondered if that piece of info was the worst-kept secret in the neighborhood. Sam must have seen it on my face.

"No, really. I haven't told anyone, but I'm telling you because it might help us. You never know."

Sure, kid. You never know. It was all I could do to not eye-roll as her story became more and more outrageous. We stood quietly and watched a crane operator hoist slabs of marble up to the fifteenth floor.

A man in a uniform pushed through the large glass door and held it open. Simultaneously, a sleek black Mercedes pulled out of the garage and the attendant got out. An elegant man dressed in a camel coat walked out the service entrance, nodded at the doorman, got into the car, and drove away.

Sam stared at the doorman. "Good, that's the new guy on duty. He won't know all the rules."

"Can you show me where that car comes out and merges into the traffic?" I asked.

"Follow me." She took a few steps and leaned her bike against the building. It now stood hidden between the wall and a vehicle next to us.

We hoofed down the alley and stepped onto west 58th Street just as the black Mercedes pulled out. I spotted a couple more cameras covering the front of the building.

"Keep your head down a little, there are cameras over there. Let's look in those shop windows across the street and not stare at your building."

"Where do you want to go? Isn't this slowing us down?" Her voice had a slightly irritated edge.

"Before we go inside," I said, "I want to know all the escape routes. Come on, let's take a look down this driveway since the Mercedes came out this way."

We slowly strolled along, and I realized that every side of the building had cameras. We made our way to the next alley and reached the back in time to see another truck drive in and park next to a van from a Jersey car wash.

Something continued to nag at me, like I was missing an important piece of information, and I'd learned to pay attention to that feeling.

"Sam, I'm not getting a good vibe about this. Are you sure you're telling me everything?"

"Of course, I am."

"Look, I can't just waltz in there with the doorman and other staff—"

"Like I said, it's the new guy on duty and he's just trying to keep it all straight. Plus, your socks match and your teeth are brushed. You look the part. Just do your rich lady thing and rush by. When you get out of the elevator on the thirty-ninth, if someone stops you as you try to go up to my floor, just tell them you're part of the design team like we planned and that you're dropping something off with a friend."

She and I looked down at the Louis Vuitton duffle, my hand gripping the handles, and she unzipped it partially. She positioned the orange Hermès scarf box so that one end stuck out of the bag a little.

I tugged the bag away from her. "So, when I get up on the forty-second floor, where do I go?"

"It's the one on the left," Sam said, now starting to sound hyped up again.

"That's kind of vague—"

"There are only two apartments on the forty-second floor," she snapped.

The young woman's tone came across as overly impatient. *Why rush?*

"I'll be on the lookout behind the building," she said. "Text me once you get there. Here's the key." She placed it in the palm of my hand.

"You know, this is kind of crazy." *How in the world did I let myself get roped into this?* "It's not too late to change our minds—"

"Are you really gonna bail on me now?" she asked, sounding annoyed. "Remember, you're the one who caused my crash. And *you're* the one who offered to help."

"I've changed my mind." I didn't mean to, but I knew my voice had taken on a curt tone.

"Why?" she almost screeched at me.

"Because it's breaking and entering, and that's a

34

crime. No way. I could lose my license at the very least."

"You owe me," she insisted. "You know, you hurt my arm!"

"And I'm sorry, I didn't mean to. But it was an accident. I don't have to repay you with a felony B&E." I stared at her. "Anyway, I don't think you're giving me the straight story."

"Are you accusing me of lying?" Sam straightened up as if insulted.

"Yes, I am. I can't accept a job where I don't know the real story." I handed back her key, which she reluctantly took.

Sam paused for a moment and nervously looked around.

"Okay, you win." She practically spit the words at me. "It's not my apartment. It belongs to my cousin, the one I got the message from when I fell trying not to crash into you. You're right. She's in trouble, and I need to get the bag." She looked up at the sky in exasperation. "I can't explain, I just have to."

"Nope," I snapped. "Not doing it. And you're foolish to try. You need to call the police." I turned on my heel to leave.

"Fine, then if you won't help me, I'll go in by myself." Sam marched across to the back entrance and parked her bike in the rack under the portico over the door.

"No, Sam, wait." I chased after her, thinking of my daughters in her desperate shoes.

She rushed inside and walked through the cavernous foyer. She waved at the man behind the desk, whom she appeared to know.

"I just need to see Marissa upstairs…" She swept by him as if she owned the place.

I watched this scene through the massive glass doors, and the doorman looked at me quizzically. I said, "I'm with her," and walked into a world of high ceilings and spaces defined by grey and cream striated marble, pale wood, crystalline-patterned stone, and tinted glass filtering the light. For a moment, I felt as if I'd jumped ahead into the twenty-second century.

Earth to Ronnie! Snap out of it. I quickly refocused and saw Sam enter an elevator. By this time, I was passing the front desk, and the man behind it looked at me slightly bewildered. "I'm with her to see Marissa, too." I gave him a little fake-attitude in my ladies-who-lunch outfit and made a beeline for the elevator before he could react.

My timing was perfect, and I sailed right in past two other people and Sam into the back of the lift, a futuristic cocoon featuring many of the same sleek materials used in the lobby.

"Twenty-seven, please," came the man's voice.

"Thirty-nine," Sam said. My head snapped slightly and I opened my mouth to say "Forty-two," but she twitched her head slightly and shot me a look.

"Thirty-nine, please," I said confidently.

The door closed, and our little space ship took off for the sky.

CHAPTER FOUR

Wow, they need to work on security in this building, I thought as my eyes swept the interior of the elevator. *I guess with all the construction, people can easily slip in and out.*

The well-dressed, middle-aged couple in the elevator spoke to each other in quiet voices. Sam looked at me, and I gave her a very slight nod, as if we agreed to not speak during the ride up to Marissa's. She looked tense, her clenched jaw. I could relate. Winging it like this was causing my anxiety level to rise, too.

What do I really know about Samantha James? Could this be a set-up of some kind? If something bad were to happen, how would anyone even know to look for me here?

Stopping suddenly on the twenty-fifth floor did nothing to calm me. The elevator door opened and revealed an empty, unfinished shell of an apartment with paper and tarps covering various surfaces, scattered construction tools and materials, and a dozen workers busy around the place.

A dust-covered, stocky, olive-skinned man in his forties with a salt-and-pepper scruff on his face and dark hair covered by a hardhat attempted to enter. The elevator man stepped in front of him. "No way. This elevator is only residents. Use the freight elevator."

The man protested. "Not working—"

"Then use the stairs." The door slid shut, and we continued moving up.

No one said a word.

We stopped on two more floors so the doorman could leave packages and where I saw more empty apartments with unfinished walls and tools and workers. *This place must be spooky once everyone goes home*, I thought as we continued skyward.

We got out on thirty-nine, leaving the couple and elevator man behind. Several workers were framing a wall that would divide the foyer from the rest of the apartment. Sam feigned surprise when they looked at us, and quickly glanced at the elevator lights that showed it continuing up.

"Shoot, we got out too early," she said to no one in particular and darted into the emergency exit hallway. I followed, and we ran up three flights of stairs to the forty-second floor. On the way up, I put on a pair of leather gloves I had in my tote. I didn't want to leave any fingerprints around the apartment I was about to enter.

We cracked open the door on the forty-second floor. This wasn't a regular high-rise hallway, but rather resembled a spacious rectangular foyer with two imposing doors at opposite ends. Several more modest service doors lined the walls on either side of the elevator.

"Have you even been here before?" I asked quietly, looking around without being too obvious.

"Sure, lots of times. I have a key, remember?" Sam said.

"Don't look at any of the cameras, and keep your head down in case the building has them in the hall. Wait here a moment."

First, I checked out the service doors. One was for the trash and recycling and the other appeared to be a janitor's closet. The third was the emergency exit stairway we'd just climbed, and I waved at Sam to come with me.

I walked up to Marissa's door to listen for voices and stood there for a moment. Nothing. Everything sounded quiet.

Oh, the hell with it. I needed to know the lay of the land up here and what my options were in case things went south fast. I rang the doorbell, gave it thirty seconds, and rang again. Nobody came to the door, and I didn't hear anyone moving around inside.

I knocked tentatively. I waited a moment and knocked again. No one answered. Sam handed me her key and I opened the door.

We entered a foyer the size of the entire first floor of my small house in New Jersey.

"Hello?" I called out, just to be sure no one was

there. I didn't hear anyone moving around the apartment or any other mysterious noises.

"Marissa," Sam called out. "Natalia, are you here?"

A child's backpack lay open on the floor with a few school items scattered next to it. Sam rushed over. "This is Natalia's pack." Her voice cracked. "She's Marissa's younger sister."

My eyes swept the walls, and what I saw put me on alert.

"The cameras inside the apartment are smashed. Why haven't the people downstairs been alerted or come up to check it out?"

"The cameras are phony," Sam said. "Nobody's coming."

"How do you know?" I asked as I walked into the living room.

"You don't know Marissa's dad," she answered. "If you think he's going to have this apartment wired into the building's security system with real cameras and everything, forget it. Not happening."

"Let's stay together in here," I said.

I walked over to a wall of glass, one of three in the immense room, practically putting my nose against the floor-to-ceiling window. I looked around at the other skyscrapers surrounding this building, the sweep of the enormous park, and Harlem further north. To the left I gazed at the George Washington Bridge off in the distance, linking New Jersey to the city.

"Wow," I said in a hushed tone, then adding, "A view to die for."

The next stop was a streamlined office, although at first glance you could have fooled me. It contained a washed walnut piece that was more table than any traditional file-drawer desk. Only one drawer was tucked underneath each end of the wood surface. An elegant brown leather and chrome highbacked swivel chair sat at the center of the desk. Those two pieces of furniture and the spectacular Central Park view through more floor-to-ceiling windows were the sum of the room's contents and setting. The desktop was completely clean—no paperwork, files, or desk accessories that were usually seen on a work space.

I walked to several switches on the one non-glass wall in the room. Six-foot-high panels of raised bookcase edges and book spines all in white covered the wall's surface. *Stunning*, I thought, almost forgetting why I was there. I flicked the switches.

Nothing happened.

Sam waved me over, and I followed her through a short hall. We entered the master bedroom and stopped. The room had been searched. All the closet doors were open, and shoe boxes were pulled out and emptied. Expensive Italian loafers and moccasins lay scattered across the floor as if they'd been flung in different directions. Bureau drawers were open, some completely pulled out and lying upside down on the bed and the floor. Socks had been pulled apart and tossed aside.

"Someone left in a hurry," I mumbled to myself, careful not to touch anything.

I glanced over at a chest of drawers with a large color photograph in a silver frame. I picked up the eight-by-ten picture and looked closer. "Whoa. It's that man who's always in the papers." It showed a man with a toddler and an elementary school-aged girl. "Why are we in Maxim Popov's apartment?"

Oh my god. It couldn't be. Things were getting worse by the second.

I stared straight at Sam. "I really need you to tell me this isn't his apartment."

She swallowed, closed her eyes, and nodded slightly.

"You brought me, under pretense, up to Maxim Popov's apartment?" I looked more closely at the somewhat dated photo and pointed at the older girl in the picture. "Is this your cousin, Marissa, a few years ago?"

Sam swallowed again and nodded yes.

"What were you thinking?" I was ready to explode. She knew it and stepped back, but I wasn't finished. "You get out of here, now! All I need is Popov's men or the police showing up here with you in the apartment—"

"But, but—"

"I'll find the bag." I looked around frantically. "Point me in the right direction."

"Down that hall, second door on the right. After Natalia's room."

"Okay, get out! Now! Go!"

Sam scooted out as fast as she could.

"And don't look up at any cameras," I called after her.

I reentered the hall and followed Sam's instructions to find Marissa's room. Along the way I glanced through the open door into Natalia's lovely room. What immediately caught my eye was a silver-framed black-and-white picture sitting on a dresser. It was of an eight or nine-year-old girl leaning against a woman, probably her mother, who had lovingly wrapped her arms around the girl. The woman looked into the camera with a serious expression while her daughter gazed up at her adoringly. I noticed the mother's eyes, and there was no disguising the pain in them. It was an extraordinary picture and I snapped a copy with my phone camera.

I had to stay focused and continued down the hall. Unlike the tossed master bedroom, Marissa's room was the epitome of tidiness. Beautiful furniture and art created a sense of calm. No fast run to IKEA to create a teenaged girl's room. Clearly, a decorator had done both girls' rooms. This one looked ready for a photo shoot. There was nothing personal about it except for another silver-framed photograph of a girl and a different beautiful woman, perhaps her mother. I snapped another picture. I planned to ask Sam for details.

I walked over to the closet as Sam had instructed, stepped inside, and turned on the light. With my gloved hands, I rummaged around the bottom of two shelves filled with sweaters. And there it was, a worn blue canvas messenger bag. I opened it enough to see it was stuffed with papers and envelopes and then quickly snapped it shut. I couldn't explain it, but I also grabbed a baggy, dark green hoodie from one of the shelves. I took off my Burberry coat, stuffed that in my own tote, and slipped the hoodie over my clothing. An instinct was telling me to look different on my way out of this building.

Samantha had told me the apartment's floor plan was somewhat spherical, so I circled back to the front via the kitchen. As I stepped into a space large enough to service a good-sized restaurant, I stopped cold. It looked like a tornado had swept through.

At first glance, nothing was where it belonged. All the cupboard doors and drawers had been opened and the contents dispersed across the countertops, floor, and breakfast table. The refrigerator had been pulled away from the wall. What had they been looking for? Did they find it? Was this mess tied to the messenger bag I'd just taken from Marissa's room?

"Watch where you step, Ronnie," I muttered as I walked among kitchen utensils and pots and pans scattered across the floor. Blood on the island countertop caught my eye. Looking down at the glint of broken glass on the floor, I squatted to get a closer look at blood on a few of the shards.

An odd sight caught my eye, this time to the right of the sink. Someone had tipped over a container of flour, leaving behind fingerprints as he tried to scoop it up—definitely a weird move. This didn't look like a group of professionals.

Taking care not to touch or step on anything in case the police ended up coming here later, I took a closer look at the prints by the sink. They were very clear, and I snapped pictures with my phone, just in case.

To the left of the sink in a corner, a broken vintage Mickey Mouse cookie jar lay on its side. All of the cookies had been dumped out on the counter. I wondered if it was time to call security so they could take a look, but a humming sound interrupted my thoughts.

I followed the sound to a laundry room off the kitchen. The machines in the laundry room were quiet, but the noise was louder. I opened a door into a smaller room and saw several computers, printers, scanners, and other equipment. The printer on a small desk was kicking out pages in a language I couldn't identify. I pulled the drawers open to find them stuffed with files. These weren't in English either, maybe a Slavic language of some sort. I closed the drawer and left.

I made my way back through the kitchen and butler's pantry into the dining room before I hit pay dirt. With my attention focused on juggling my tote, the Vuitton duffle, and the messenger bag, I almost tripped over a floor lamp that lay on its side. The momentum threw me forward, where I tripped again, this time over a corner of the rug that was flipped up. I threw my hands out to break my fall, and two of my bags tumbled off my shoulders and to the floor. From my floor's-eye-view, I noticed two chairs standing back-to-back at one corner of the long table and blood stains on the rug.

"What's going on here?" I stood up.

There were scuff marks on the floor, as if the chairs had been dragged across the wood. Why would someone have needed those chairs?

My cell phone rang, and I picked up. "What?"

There was silence on the other end of the phone.

Anger crept into my voice. "You know more about this than you've told me."

Sam simply asked, "Do you have the bag? You have to get out of there, Ronnie."

"Son of a bitch, you lied to me. Is your name even Samantha James?"

"Yes, I swear."

"Or are you a Popov, too, and more than a cousin? Seriously, this is a police matter—"

"Please don't call them! Come down and I'll explain everything."

"First, I'm putting the bag back where I found it—"

The sound of the front door opening and two male voices arguing stopped me cold.

CHAPTER FIVE

One voice in the foyer sounded nervous and young. Another more imposing voice responded.

I didn't move, but I could see them heading for the office that had only a desk. I hastily backtracked to the pantry, pulled the hoodie up to cover my hair, and almost got the door shut before the man entered.

Hugging my three bulky bags tighter, I peeked out a little. I recognized the dusty workman from earlier, the same stocky, mid-forties, olive-skinned man with dark hair underneath the hardhat who'd tried to board the elevator when I was coming up. He rubbed the grey-flecked scruff on his face as he looked around.

The voice from the office called out, "*Pasaporte?*"

This guy yelled back, "No."

He pulled open the freezer drawer in the monstrous Sub-Zero refrigerator. First, he rummaged around and then, in frustration, began emptying the drawer's contents. He tossed the rock-hard food in every direction. The frozen food thudded and slid across the floor before skidding to a stop.

I tried to snap a couple of photos with my phone through the crack of the open door.

A skinny, younger man—probably early twenties—in a black hoodie over a tee-shirt with an olive knit cap on his head appeared in the doorway. Again, his tone was nervous as he spoke. I grabbed a few more pictures.

The man in the hardhat cut him off and went back to what he was doing.

"José," the younger man whined.

"Tomás!" the man in the hardhat barked. He said something, but the only word I could understand was *pasaportes.*

The chastised man in the black hoodie left, mumbling something. Ignoring him, José went back to work searching the freezer.

Several minutes later, José slammed the freezer drawer shut and looked around the huge kitchen. He zeroed in on the pantry and strode toward my hiding place. Rather than wait to be caught cowering in the corner of this closet, I grabbed my pepper spray out of my tote.

When José was close enough to look inside, I hurled myself as hard as I could against the door. Using the explosive move to my advantage, I rolled myself out of the closet like a spinning top, one of my bags slamming into his face. The move tossed him back and off-balance, giving me just enough time to rotate past him and out of his reach. My arm came around and I sprayed him full blast in the eyes with the pepper spray.

He covered his face with his one arm, the other grasping at the air, trying to connect with me. He stumbled on a frozen steak and his feet flew out from under him.

I sprinted across the kitchen, dodging left and right to avoid other frozen foods scattered on the floor. I shot through the dining room into the foyer. I could hear José yelling, while Tomás yelled something back.

I blasted out of the apartment and through the door to the service area with the emergency stairway. I ran down two flights to fortieth floor and stopped. No one was following me yet, so I walked down the final flight to thirty-nine and glanced at the same construction workers I'd seen on the way up. I pressed the elevator button and gave them a quick nod.

The doors opened and I looked over my shoulder. Thank goodness, the men had already lost interest in me and were back at work.

A different elevator man greeted me, and I stepped in, miraculously still in possession of my tote, the Louis Vuitton duffle, and the blue messenger bag. As we rode down to the back lobby, I pulled the hoodie off and stuffed it and the messenger bag inside my tote.

I walked out of the building casually. The two men had not seen me in the apartment and wouldn't recognize me should they show up. Still, my heart was pounding from the encounter upstairs.

My first order of business was to find Samantha. I was fuming, but I couldn't tell if I was angrier at her for getting me into this or at myself for rushing in without getting all the facts first. I'd felt so guilty about her bike crash that I didn't do my usual due diligence when she called. I had only myself to blame for being in the middle of this mess.

And now I'd just broken into a mobster's apartment to remove a bag full of papers and beat up a home invader before escaping.

Ronnie, when will you learn? I glanced down at the messenger bag Samantha had sent me in for. Maybe *this* is what he wanted?

I looked around and saw Sam waving at me from the corner of a huge truck parked in the back. I marched over. "You have more explaining to do—"

"I promise to tell you everything," she pleaded, stepping back so we wouldn't be seen.

"Two guys came into the apartment looking for something. Passports, they said." I showed her the pictures on my phone, and added, "I barely got out of that apartment in one piece."

Sam held up her phone, and there was a picture of the same guy, the one with the hardhat. She said, "He's the driver of the van over there."

"That car wash van?"

"Yeah. I got pictures of the logo and phone number on the side and back."

Instead of where it had first been next to the construction trucks, the vehicle was now parked in front of the special escape exit in the other building that Sam had referred to earlier.

At that moment, the man with the hardhat and the younger guy with the hoodie walked out of the back lobby of the tower. The man with the hardhat coughed non-stop, pausing here and there to catch his breath and drink from a water bottle. My pepper spray had been an effective weapon.

"Hey, there they are. How did they get down here so fast," I said more to myself than Sam. "They must have hopped onto the freight elevator."

"Like I said, the man with the hardhat, he's the driver," Sam declared.

"I think his name is José. And the guy with the hoodie is Tomás," I said. "I heard them using their names upstairs when they searched the place."

As the two men walked toward the van, José sent a text. By the time they got there and had walked to the other side of the vehicle, the exit door had opened and a couple of guys hustled out two people. It was hard to see much because the van blocked our view. The men were arguing as one of them came around to the driver's side and hopped in.

Suddenly, there was a scuffle and we heard two muffled female voices. One sounded young.

Sam inhaled quickly. "That's Natalia and Marissa. I'm sure of it."

Before I could say anything, the van door slammed shut. The driver hopped in, started the engine, and took off down the alley between the buildings before turning onto 58th Street.

CHAPTER SIX

"They've definitely got them," Sam's voice shook. She tugged on my arm, pleading, "Please, we've got to follow them."

Damn! I shook my head in exasperation. My car wasn't right here for us to jump in and pursue them. I hurriedly started walking.

"Marissa and Natalia are the only family I've got." She grabbed her bicycle and followed, sniffling and wiping away the tears.

"You're sure you've got good pictures of the van's logo and name?"

Sam nodded. "Yes, yes."

"Let's go." Already ahead of her, I added, "My car's around the corner."

"Can I put my bike in the back of your car?"

"It's an SUV, so yeah. Come on." I looked over my shoulder at her. "And call the police. Right now!"

"What?"

"Call 911 right now." As we hurried down the street to the garage, I glanced back again. "While I get my car, give your pictures of the van and the kidnappers to the police."

"We know where to go," she shot back. "We don't need the police."

"They have more resources to go after them than we do."

"No, we can't call the cops," she argued. "It's too risky. When it comes to Maxim Popov, you don't call the police."

"That's crazy." I nodded my head to the left toward a ramp. "And I still want to know why you sent me into Maxim Popov's apartment."

We rushed down the ramp into the garage.

"I promise to explain everything." There was desperation in Sam's eyes. "All I know is right now Marissa and Natalia are in that van."

"How does that crew even know about that side exit? You said only the residents knew about it." I paid the attendant.

Sam shrugged. "Somebody in the building must have talked."

The car was nearby, so we dashed over to get it. She put her bike in the back of my Jeep.

"Where are we going in Paterson?" I asked. "Please find out if there's more than one of those car washes."

We got into the car, and I pulled out of the garage, heading west. Sam tapped quickly on her phone and got to work.

It turned out there were actually five Super Lux Car

Washes around Paterson. While she put the addresses in her phone's GPS, I maneuvered the SUV as fast as I could along the Westside Highway heading north. I watched for the car wash van as I drove, but they must have gotten enough of a head start, and I didn't spot them anywhere.

A car swerved in front and I hit the brakes. "Watch out, mister."

Sam continued working on her phone, and things were awfully quiet in the seat next to me for a while. Finally, her fingers stopped tapping.

"Look, we've got at least a half hour or more before we get to Paterson. Seems like a good time to talk." I moved into the left lane and picked up some speed.

Sam volunteered nothing. She just stared straight ahead and chewed on her lower lip.

"Exactly what are you and the sisters mixed up in?"

"I promised Marissa I'd never tell."

"Why did you really want to go into the apartment?" Still no response as I merged into the lane for the George Washington Bridge. "Why did you want me to get that bag?"

"Look, you offered to help when I got that text. I just took you up on it. You were the one who said you could help me. Not the other way around. It was as simple as that—"

"What about the text you received?" I interrupted.

"I can't tell you."

"If I'm going to help you, truly, I need to know what's going on here."

"I'm trying to decide how much I can tell you—"

"What do you mean, how much you can tell me?" I interjected. "Try telling me everything."

"—in order to keep Marissa and Natalia safe."

I picked up speed on the bridge. "Their dad's a mob boss, four guys grabbed them in their apartment. Maybe they're on their way to Paterson, or maybe they're going to end up in the Hudson."

Sam burst into tears.

"Sorry, I didn't mean to paint such a hopeless picture." I toned things down and spoke more softly. "You asked for my help, so I need to know as much as possible." I handed Sam a packet of tissues.

She blew her nose. "I got that text right after I almost crashed into you. I can't show it to you while you're driving, but it says 'HELP.'"

"That's all? From what we saw, she and her sister were taken against their will," I said. "Someone's kidnapped them."

Sam's tears started again and her voice quivered. "Maybe they're forcing her to come with them or they'll hurt Natalia."

"Let's not get ahead of ourselves. What does a kidnapping have to do with you wanting that bag?"

"A while back, Marissa made me promise that if anything ever happened to her, I'd do whatever it takes to get that blue bag for her."

"What's in it?

"I don't know—"

"I don't buy that."

"Let me finish," she exclaimed.

I stayed quiet for the moment. We drove off the bridge and into Fort Lee, New Jersey.

"Like I said before, I don't know what's in that blue bag." Sam stared at her phone. "She just said she'd been collecting information, important papers, that would guarantee her safety."

"Her safety from what?"

She took a deep breath and let it out slowly. "I swear, I don't know. She said it was better if I didn't know."

"What about Natalia? What about her safety?"

"It would protect her safety, too."

"What about you?" I asked Sam.

"What do you mean, what about me?"

"Wouldn't it protect you, too? You're part of the family—" I hit the brakes. "God, I hate these huge trucks that just bully in front of you because of their size. Where are the cops when you need them?"

I thought I heard a quiet moan come from Sam. I let her be while I tried to figure out our next move, and then she surprised me by piping up.

"Look, Marissa and Natalia are *like* my family. They're all I've got. They're in trouble and we've got to find them. End of story."

"You know, unless we get lucky, we're going to have to call the police."

But Sam wasn't finished. "Everyone knows you

don't mess with Popov, so we can't call the police."

"We may not have a choice."

"Alright," Sam grumbled. "But I hope we find them soon."

Her phone beeped and she looked down.

"Who's that? Another text from Marissa?"

"No, just junk. Maybe I should text her back?" Sam tapped her phone. "So that she knows someone is looking for her?"

"We shouldn't text her. I don't want them to know she has a phone."

After twenty more minutes on I-80, we finally reached the first exits for the city of Paterson. We took the one that the GPS said would lead us to the closest car wash on our list.

I wasn't sure where we were heading or what we would find in a town that I knew little about. My second-hand impressions that Paterson had more than its share of inner-city crime, drugs, corruption, and poverty were admittedly uninformed. Whatever the reality, if the car wash didn't pan out, I wasn't sure how we'd track down the four men who'd kidnapped Sam's friends, let alone find the sisters.

We arrived at the first car wash on the outskirts of town. I guided my dusty SUV around the building while Sam discreetly took pictures.

"Platinum fifteen-dollars, gold twelve, silver ten, bronze eight," a short brown-haired man said. He wore a black Super Lux Car Wash tee-shirt that stretched over the beginnings of a beer belly under his unzipped parka. Without waiting for my response, he went ahead and called out instructions to a co-worker in Spanish.

I chose and paid for the cheapest. I didn't know how many more Super Lux facilities I'd have to visit for a wash before hopefully tracking down the kidnappers.

My attempt at casual chit-chat as he guided my SUV onto the track didn't work at all. He seemed uptight, glancing around as if he were watching for someone.

One of his co-workers yelled to him in accented English, "Phone call from boss."

As soon as the track pulled my car into the wash tunnel, the man slipped into the office to take the call.

The spray and soap and brushes pounded my SUV so loudly that I could barely hear myself think.

I leaned in toward Sam. "I haven't seen our guys yet. Have you?"

She shook her head no.

"Start at the beginning. How do you know the sisters? How far back do you go?"

"Marissa and I met each other at a club in the city—"

"So you haven't known each other that long," I commented.

"Actually, we've known each other since we were fifteen."

"Okay, how did that work? You know, meeting at a club when you were fifteen."

"We happened to stand next to each other in line

with friends. We were hoping to get past the guys at the door, and that they wouldn't notice that we were too young." Sam chuckled. "If you're a group of girls, you always have a better shot."

"Did you get into this club?" I ask.

"Do you even have to ask?" she retorted. "Of course, we got in. Anyway, we had fun and we clicked. We started hanging out, and pretty soon we were on our way to BFFs."

"Friends meet in many different ways."

She looked at me with the saddest face. "I couldn't stand it if something happened to her and her sister."

The car wash got louder once the dryers turned on, and I had to speak up. "Why did you say they're the only family you've got?"

"Because they are." Sam spoke louder, too.

"What happened to your own family, your parents?"

"My mom died a long time ago, and I don't remember my dad." Her tone was firm, as if ordering me not to dig further. That was okay with me. There would be time later to learn more.

"Tell me about Marissa's sister. Are they close?"

"Incredibly close." Sam tilted her head. "Natalia is adorable. And Marissa is more like a cross between being a big sister and a mom."

"Where is Mrs. Popov?" I asked.

"Both of them are dead." She looked out her side window.

"Both of them?"

"Marissa's mother died when she was a little girl. Mr. Popov remarried, and they had Natalia. Her mother died a year ago."

"That must have been heart-breaking for both of them," I said. "And especially for Natalia, since it was so recent."

"Sure it was, but also for Marissa. She and her stepmom were really close," Sam said. "She even called her Mama Kate and she told me she could talk to her about everything."

"She must have been a very special woman to be a terrific mother and a great stepmother. Stepparenting isn't easy."

"Well, she was," Sam answered. "I kinda wished she'd have been my stepmom, too."

"What a loss for all of you."

"You're not kidding," Sam said. "Well, Marissa has her theories about what happened there."

"Really?" I asked. "Such as—"

"I'm finished talking about this." She looked away, staring out the passenger window.

I took a moment to digest this new information. "All right, I'll make you a deal," I said. "We'll try this rescue your way, but there's a limit. If we don't find any trace by the time we've seen the last car wash, we're going to the cops. Agreed?"

She started to protest. I put my hand up to stop her.

"Look, Sam. Kidnapping is serious. Their lives are in danger. And the police can bring more resources to finding them. Agreed?"

She closed her eyes and exhaled. She opened them a second later and stared right at me. "Okay. Agreed."

As we came to the end, two men hand-dried the moisture that still remained on the front windshield. Neither of them was part of the group at the tower.

I put my car into gear, rolled down the window, and dropped a tip into the large barrel. The one closest said in a quiet voice, "*Gracias*."

"Mostly Latinos working here," Sam commented, and we drove off.

It was the same story at the next car wash. Four to six men worked at the site, and none were in the mood to talk.

At the third one, I changed my approach and opted for a hand-wash. Looking around while they washed my car, I noticed that no one wore any protective eye or hand gear or waterproof clothing on this chilly November day. I wondered if that was typical of most car washes—maybe not.

Like the other locations, the workers seemed withdrawn and not open to friendly conversation. None of them wanted to handle money. There was always just one guy at each site who handled the cash. Finally, the price of the hand wash, which was more labor intensive than the automatic washes, was too good to be true.

As we pulled up to the fourth Super Luxe, Sam and I recognized one of the guys who had come back to Max Popov's apartment. A backwards ball cap had replaced his construction helmet, and he now also wore a black tee shirt with the car wash logo under an open fleece jacket as he walked up to the office to go on duty.

"That's him! That's the guy from her apartment. Go get him, Ronnie!"

"He might recognize me. Let me do it my way."

I parked my SUV, got out, and attempted to talk with the other workers at this car wash. One hefty-looking guy sat to the side with his nose in a *New York Post*.

"I'd like to get information on detailing my car," I said to a boyish-looking worker. He nodded toward the boss.

I smiled at him. "How's it going today?"

He looked at me, surprised that I was addressing him, and responded quietly, "Good."

The big guy with the *New York Post* quickly looked up and bellowed, "No talking with customers." He rolled up the paper.

The shy young man started to say something, but the boss-man slapped the paper against the wall and cut him off with a threatening tone. The worker went mute. Sam and I glanced at each other.

I walked over to the boss and asked him about detailing my SUV and the price.

"No detailing."

"What do you mean, no detailing?" I asked.

"Platinum fifteen dollars, gold twelve, silver ten, bronze eight," he said, repeating the price list I'd heard earlier.

"Got it." I pulled out my money. "I'd like a bronze."

I hopped back into the car and for the fourth time got the Jeep washed. I noticed a row of windows that fronted a hallway alongside the washing area. The windows had been white-washed to prevent looking through them. This car wash wasn't state-of-the-art and looked dated and rundown.

As we came out the other end, Sam slid down in her seat and put her shades on. José began drying the windshield. Trying not to stare, I got a good close look at him. Having worn a hoodie during our kitchen altercation at the tower, I didn't think he'd recognize me through the tinted windshield of my car.

We rolled forward, I put the SUV in gear, and we turned onto the street. I drove two blocks, turned around in a grocery store parking lot, and drove back, pulling into a curbside space at an angle to the building that gave us a good view of the car wash front and back.

"Now, was there anything out of the ordinary about that message you got from Marissa?"

"If either of us ever sends it, the other one drops everything to help," Sam said. "It was actually a Snap. And those disappear after you open them. But I took a screen shot to save it before it did." She caught my look of confusion. "It's all part of this app called Snapchat."

While we sat in the SUV, an erratic stream of vehicles drove up to the back of the car wash—everything from a tiny Chevrolet Cruze to a midsize Honda Accord to a large Chevy Impala. The parade included minivans, SUVs, and even a small Ford pickup truck. The colors mostly spanned a rainbow of shades of white to grey to black, except for one sleek, bright red Corvette. Some were shiny and well-cared for and some not, but all were at various stages of needing a wash. Most of the cars were in decent shape.

That all held true until I noticed a filthy, beat-up beige minivan with a dent on the passenger door. A supersize black SUV, like a Suburban, stayed close behind the van's bumper, almost crowding the minivan. One of the employees blocked any other cars from pulling up. Meanwhile, two other cars exited at the end of the wash and left.

Both the minivan and SUV scooted onto the track and disappeared into the innards of the car wash.

CHAPTER SEVEN

"*Amigo!*" the guy in charge yelled, and José threw his towel to the side, moved around the outside of the building, and ended up at the entrance to the wash. The boss went inside. José never took his eyes off the man.

A moment later, he nodded to him and pressed a button off to the side of the control board. Blue doors rolled down to close both ends of the car wash.

Things appeared to come to a pause, and the employee holding back the cars in line let everyone know they would be back in operation momentarily. With that guy distracted, José pulled a couple of bills out of the cash box and hastily stuffed them into his back pocket.

"What's going on there?"

"I don't know, but it's definitely weird." Sam checked her phone.

"Any new Snaps from Marissa?" I asked.

"Nothing."

"Hmmm. Maybe they found her phone and took it away from her." I paused. "Or maybe the battery died."

"Should I go for it and Snap her now?"

"Not yet," I answered. "Let's give her a little more time."

I kept my eyes on the building, determined to watch this play out. Pretty soon the doors rolled open and the brushes and dryers were back in operation. José came around the outside of the building, picked up his towels and started drying the minivan's windshield. It rolled out slowly, and José switched his focus to drying the windows on the black SUV. The cars in line began entering the car wash, while the beat-up beige van and black SUV drove off.

Something was definitely off here.

"Are we just going to sit here?" Sam asked, sounding a bit whiny. "Why don't we get out and do some real detective work to find Marissa and Natalia."

"And what would you suggest we do? Where we should go?"

"Shouldn't we drive around and look for them?" Exasperation came through in her tone of voice.

"There are a lot of streets in Paterson. We only know there's a connection to this car wash chain and that guy José who's wiping down the wet cars. And *you* don't want to call the police," I said. "So where do you want to start?"

Sam didn't say a word. She just stared at me.

"Also, the kidnappers probably have them tied up inside a building somewhere, and we'd have to—"

"Okay, okay, I get it." She folded her arms across

her front and gave a loud sigh.

"Sam, this is called surveillance and it's big piece of the private investigator's tool kit. It may be boring, but patience during surveillance can break open a case."

About fifteen minutes later, the beige minivan with its dented passenger door was back. Right on its tail, a dark red minivan with a few dents and scrapes of its own followed it. Sam and I watched once again as two vehicles entered the car wash and an employee held up the drivers waiting in line. The boss went inside before José closed the doors. Four or five minutes later, everything started up again as the two vehicles drove off in different directions.

I sat quietly, trying to figure out what to make of these pauses at the car wash.

Sam checked her phone and fidgeted. "What's next?"

"I don't know yet," I said.

"You don't know?" Sam threw up her arms. "Are you any good at this?"

"If you're not happy with the way I work, you have two choices. Call the police right now, as I advised—"

"No!" she almost screeched.

"—or find someone else. Get on your phone and see if you can find some other PI in Paterson."

"And start all over with someone new? No way. What I need is for you to do something," she demanded.

"What we really need is for José to put down his towels and head back to where he came from before he went on duty, and that could take a while depending upon his shift. Do I think something else is going on at this car wash? Yes, but I'm not sure it necessarily helps us find Marissa and Natalia." I looked back over my shoulder down the street. "I thought I saw a coffee shop two blocks back when we turned around. While I sit here keeping a close watch, why don't you get yourself a coffee?"

Sam looked at me funny but she took my advice. She even surprised me when she returned with one for me, too. We both sat quietly, just sipping and watching.

"Still nothing from Marissa?" I asked.

Sam shook her head no and showed me her phone.

"It's time to reach out. May I?" I asked and she handed it over. *I hope this doesn't get Marissa killed once they know we're onto her.*

I nervously tapped the message.

-Where are you?

I hit *Send* and looked up. "The van is back."

The beige van with the dent in the door returned for a third time. An eggplant-colored SUV coming from the opposite direction quickly pulled right in behind it. They waited patiently in line as two other vehicles went through the car wash.

Sam and I continued watching. When the van and SUV got to the front, the drivers didn't pay. The boss just waved them in. As the other worker told the drivers in line that it would be a few moments while they checked something inside, José once again came out a door next to the end of the car wash. He hightailed it back to the boss's station at the beginning of the wash. The boss moved inside the building while José awaited his signal.

This time I was ready. "Wait for me here, Sam."

I slipped out of my car and walked casually toward the building. Suddenly the car wash doors at front and back dropped down. Now that I was nearer the building, I could also hear the sound of the machinery quieting down inside.

I tried the knob of the door José had used; it turned easily in my hand, so I carefully pushed it open just enough to squeeze inside and crouch down. The space was dark, but there was enough light coming through the whitewashed window. The streaky brushstrokes left plenty of spaces on the glass where one could peak through.

I looked around my hiding place. This had been a long gallery where people could watch vehicles progress through the car wash. Now it wasn't in use anymore.

I crab walked closer to the window and peeked through the glass. I could see everything, and nobody appeared to be looking in my direction. Straightaway, I looked around the space in general—up at the ceiling, the walls, the lighting, the equipment—but nothing gave me pause.

Since I was at the end where the cars exited, my angle let me look toward the front of the minivan and the SUV behind it. The beige van's dented door was now open, and four bulky, rough-looking guys were pulling three women out of the van. The women—two of them probably in their twenties or late-teens and the third maybe in her early forties—had their hands tied together in back. They were crying and pleading, but the men put their hands over the women's mouths and talked to them, maybe telling them to quiet down. The boss watched everything from the back where the cars entered. I needed to be careful that he didn't spot me in here.

I took pictures of both the women, the men, and the vehicles. The youngest had a long, black, stringy pony tail, wore jeans, sneakers, a striped tank top, and had on a pink puffy jacket. The other young woman wore black leggings, white sneakers, a blue tunic-length shirt, and a navy wind breaker on top, hardly warm enough for November. Her dark brown hair was pulled up in a messy bun. The older woman wore a burgundy jersey dress with white zig-zags, sensible loafers, and a cloth coat. Her black hair was cut short with one wide silver streak starting at a cowlick near the right side of her forehead. All three looked as if they had come from a factory because they wore blue work aprons.

The guys shoved the women toward the SUV. The youngest-looking sobbed uncontrollably, shaking and falling to her knees. In between gasps of air, she begged and begged, looking up at the one who appeared to be in charge. He was merciless as he grabbed her hair and forced her to stand up, causing her to cry out in pain. He jostled her toward the back seat of the SUV and pulled a zip tie from the inside pocket of his tight navy blazer jacket. As they got to the vehicle, the girl saw the zip tie and cried even harder, but he pushed her into the back seat.

I moved closer since the SUV's door blocked my view. I still couldn't see much because the guy stood in the way, but he appeared to push her onto the floor. Then he fussed with her, probably using the zip tie to secure her to the bottom hardware of the front seat.

The two other women were more resigned and compliant when the men led them to the vehicle before securing them somewhere inside the back seat. Then the man in the navy blazer opened the back of the SUV and pulled out blankets which he tossed over the three women.

At that point, the men split up. Two got into the beige minivan and two got into the SUV. The vehicles had been idling the entire time and now the driver in the van nodded to the boss in charge of the car wash. He pressed a button on the wall and the large doors opened. The two vehicles rolled out of the exit as I crouched down and carefully backed up in the hallway to get to the door.

I cracked it open in time to see both cars turning onto the main road, the beige van returning to wherever it came from. The dark eggplant SUV with the women went in the opposite direction.

I looked around to be sure no one was paying

attention at my end of the building before racing over to my car. Sam reached over to open my door; I slid in and turned on the ignition.

"Where are we going? Did you find Marissa and Natalia?" she asked.

"Give me a second," I responded. "Let me get going here."

I waited until the SUV was two blocks down the street before I pulled out to tail it. Something interesting was going on at this car wash. I had a good idea what it was, and it might even help us figure out where Sam's friends were.

CHAPTER EIGHT

Sam was shocked, clasping her hands with worry as she listened to me describe what I'd just witnessed. "Do you think that's what happened to Marissa and Natalia once they were pushed into that van?" she asked.

"Remember, we barely saw them," I cautioned. "We don't know what's actually going on with them yet."

Doing my best to keep a block-and-a-half gap between my SUV and the one with the three women, we followed them through the bustling traffic. The landscape changed from the neighborhoods of Paterson as we headed toward the suburbs.

"But they grabbed those women and forced them to go against their will," Sam insisted. "It sounds just like what happened to Marissa and Natalia."

"It certainly seems that way," I agreed. "But we need to find out more before we decide that these two situations are similar."

"Wait a minute." She put her hand on my upper arm as if she really wanted my attention. "Why did they do the hand-off inside a car wash? That is so effed up."

I glanced at her hand on my arm while I was driving and she removed it.

"Okay. Think about it. They're each in a vehicle to do the deal. These days, there are a lot of cameras everywhere. So, a car wash makes sense if you have access, and I didn't see any cameras inside when I looked around."

"That does make sense," she responded.

"I think something else is going on with these three women."

"What do you mean," Sam asked.

"We may be in the middle of a human trafficking ring."

"What?!" Sam screeched. "No way."

The whole idea was unbelievable to me, too, even though I was aware that human trafficking—both sex and labor—was big business in the United States. Now that I had witnessed the handoff inside the car wash, I wondered how many other women had been transferred from the beige van the two other times we watched it enter the car wash?

The SUV up ahead made a right turn.

"Did the guys in that car pay for those women?" Sam asked. "Do they own them? Are those women their slaves?"

"They're likely somebody's slaves, but I doubt it's those two. The men are probably working for a bigger boss," I said, making a right turn, too. "Who owns those car washes? Do you remember ever hearing Marissa's father talk about his businesses?"

"No. Maxim Popov was very private," she insisted. "He wouldn't even talk to us whenever we hung out at her apartment."

"Well, let's see where this takes us. Following him..." I nodded at the SUV, "...it's a long shot, but what do we care as long as it leads us to the sisters."

We continued to drive further and further away from the heart of Paterson into some older neighborhoods. We passed 1950s or '60s apartment buildings. Scattered between them were clusters of modest houses with small yards.

A few shops began to pop up, and we followed the car to an old strip mall. The early stages of construction at one end near a restaurant and a couple of other shops signaled the start of a facelift for the entire shopping center. A few second-tier chains populated the mall, but its tenants were mostly modest mom and pop businesses—a hair salon, a liquor store, a check cashing business, a coffee shop, and a bodega, to name a few.

I pulled into the mall parking where I had a good view of the entire strip. We watched the SUV slow down in front of Bella Vida Nail Salon. The driver tapped on his horn and a petite woman with black hair, black trousers, black flats, and a blue cardigan came out, inhaling the smoke from a cigarette between her fingers. She used her other hand to shade her face from the lunch-time sun. They talked for a moment, and she tapped the ash from her cigarette as she turned to go back inside.

The vehicle continued driving along the front of the mall, passing the other stores. Finally, it turned left to continue around the building.

I did the same and pulled over to the far sidewalk where I could watch the back of the building. It was also a good spot to take more pictures.

The two men leaned in from opposite sides of the back seat and pulled out two of the women. When the guy in the blue blazer reached in for the girl with the ponytail, she saw her chance and broke away from him. She ran as fast as she could toward us, and the guy pushed the second woman toward his partner, who now hung onto two of them. The guy in the blazer ran after the girl.

"Get down," I said as I quickly slid down in my seat. "Don't let them see us."

Rather than running closer to our car, the girl made a speedy turn and raced up the street away from the mall. She was fast, but the guy was right on her and she didn't stand a chance. About a block ahead, he finally grabbed her ponytail. She crashed down on her back, screaming loudly in pain.

He lifted her up from the pavement and slugged her jaw, her head whipping to the side. She crumpled, banging her head hard against the curb.

Sam reached for her door handle.

"Don't touch that door," I ordered, and Sam froze.

"I've got to go help that girl..." Sam looked furious.

"If you jump into the middle of that, as terrible as it

is, you will tip them off and we may never find out what's happened to Marissa and Natalia," I said. "Take a deep breath."

The girl was out cold, and the man scooped her up. I could see blood on her face and neck, probably from both the punch and the fall. He calmly walked back toward the small group standing by the salon back door.

The other women were now crying. The door opened, and the same woman we had just seen in front of the salon stepped out. All she needed was one look at the man holding the unconscious, bloody girl, and she lit into him.

"Wow, what's with her?" Sam asked, snapping pictures with her phone, too.

"Maybe she's complaining about damaged goods." It was horrifying to witness, especially when the woman handed one of the men a wad of cash. Then she let the group inside, the man carrying the limp girl bringing up the rear.

Sam and I pushed ourselves up on our seats and stared in disbelief.

"Oh, my God," Sam yowled. "I can't believe what we just saw. Was she actually paying for those women? What's going on in there?"

"I'm pretty sure that was the brutality of human trafficking. Maybe they were sold and they're being moved into another business." I continued to watch the back door they had entered. "I know it's a nail salon, but you have to wonder. The business could be legit, but it's highly doubtful when you see the way these girls were manhandled and forced to come here."

Sam put her phone on her lap. "What do we do now?"

"Well, since we're already here, maybe we can find out more before we go back to Paterson." I drove back to the front of the mall. "We can go in, get a manicure—"

"A manicure?" Sam screeched.

"It's a way to check things out in there," I said, as I parked.

She looked at me like I was crazy. "I don't wear polish."

"Even better." I flashed my unpolished nails on one of my hands at her. "We'll both go."

Sam opened the car door.

"Wait," I said, and she closed it. "We need to give them a few minutes to settle down in there." I pulled some bills out my pocket. "Go grab us each a sandwich while I watch the door. This could end up being a long night, after all."

~~~~~

A quarter of an hour later, we returned to the nail salon and entered a world of coral and pink. The place was vibrant with girl talk. A manicurist in trousers and a tailored shirt sat at one of the pedicure stations, organizing her tools. She gathered them and walked to a room in the back hallway. A customer sat at the other pedicure station with her feet soaking in warm water.

We stopped at the reception desk to request a basic manicure but the boss was on the phone. Maybe in her late-forties and prettier than I'd thought when I first saw her, she put her hand over the mouthpiece and greeted us quickly, waving us around the divider toward the manicure stations. I noticed her cell phone sitting on the desk as I grabbed a couple of business cards from a little tray.

As we came around the divider, we saw right away that the older woman in the dress and sensible shoes had already been put to work sweeping up around the salon. She put the broom away and went to the small hallway. The younger one with the leggings, sneakers, and sloppy bun was sitting at a small table, organizing bottles of nail polish. Neither had on her blue work apron anymore. There was no sign of the one with the ponytail who had been carried inside. I wondered which door she was behind as I glanced down two different hallways.

Sam and I sat down with Valentina and Emma, two middle-aged manicurists, and we chose our nail polish colors. As the women dipped our hands into a soapy solution to soften our cuticles, we pretended to carry on a lighthearted conversation about things going on at home. Sam proved to be quite adept as an actress, easily slipping into the character of a young woman from the suburbs.

As the manicurists brushed on the first coat of colored polish, a man entered the salon.

"Hello, Luciana," His voice caressed the syllables of her name.

The owner greeted him with a huge smile. "Mr. Metcalfe, so good to see you again. Right on time for your one-thirty pedicure."

Her persona had shifted immediately from all-business to one of feminine amenability, especially evident in her voice. Clearly, everything was all about service for this customer. When he looked into the shop owner's laser-focused eyes, he saw himself reflected in a way that he liked. Her accented voice acquired a slight breathiness. He was putty in her hands.

"We have your lunch ready just the way you like it." She led Mr. Metcalfe down a hallway to a private room in the back.

The older woman with the grey streak in her hair brought a tray nicely laid out for lunch. She took it in to Mr. Metcalfe, came out, and returned with a miniature carafe of white wine and a glass for him.

Suddenly the young woman who had been organizing the nail polish bottles got up and made a beeline for the bathroom. The boss stopped her.

"Hey, where do you think you're going?" Luciana demanded, her voice now harsh.

"Bathroom?" the young woman asked.

"No bathroom break. In one hour. Only two bathroom breaks a day, and you just got here."

"Please, please," she pleaded. She squeezed her legs together to show she couldn't hold it much longer.

Surprisingly, Luciana took mercy. "Okay. Go now. But no break later." She waved toward the hallway leading to the back of the building. "Use the bathroom for employees."

The phone rang, and the boss woman picked it up to help a customer make an appointment. Meanwhile, the woman headed down the hall to the back, her messy bun bouncing as she walked. A moment later, the heavy door to the back slammed.

Luciana quickly threw down the phone and jumped up, hollering for Rafael. A young man emerged from the other hall, and she gave him instructions in Spanish. He tucked his cell phone in his back pocket and went outside.

Five minutes later, the back door opened again and I heard multiple footsteps. Another door opened and closed, and a key locked it. The older woman was back sweeping, biting her lip, and surreptitiously glancing around.

Both Sam and I tried talking to our manicurists to learn more about the salon, but they didn't seem to want to converse. I smiled and nodded at a customer across from us, who was getting a pedicure.

"I wonder what's going on back there," I said in a quiet, friendly voice.

Both Valentina and Emma looked down, staying silent and concentrating on our nails, just doing their jobs. They placed our hands in small nail dryers to help the top coat dry faster.

The pedicure customer shook her head and smiled. "I don't get it. I come here all the time and it's usually so peaceful." She shrugged. "Maybe it's tough breaking in new employees."

I pulled out some money and tried to give each manicurist a tip, but the boss swooped in to retrieve it before they could pocket the bills. Luciana said in a super-sweet voice, "All tips are shared with everyone in the salon."

Sam and I went over to the cash register, and I paid. "My treat."

I made one last stab to find out about the girl with the ponytail. "I'll be right with you," I said to Sam and smiled. "Just need a little bathroom break before we leave."

"I'll wait here," she said, with a knowing look.

I hurried down the second hallway before the boss could stop me, opening all the doors under the guise of looking for a toilet.

Luciana came running after me as I opened the third door and got a glimpse of the girl. She stared up at me, surprised.

"Oh, sorry," I apologized. "Just looking for the bathroom."

The manager took me firmly by the arm. "The bathroom is this way."

She guided me roughly down the other hall to the ladies' room just as Mr. Metcalfe came out from his. I tried to peer inside the room, but Luciana pushed me ahead and shut the door as we passed by.

Once Sam and I left the salon, she tugged at my arm. "We can't just leave those women in there."

"Yes, we can. Come on, let's go. Those women aren't going anywhere, and we'll make sure that either we or the police come back for them." We got in the car, and I snapped a few more shots of the front of the salon and its signage. "I've got a lot of pictures, so we have something to show them. And I have a couple of business cards."

As we pulled out, Sam said, "I just hate leaving them there."

"I do, too. But I promise we're not going to forget about this place. Right now, our focus is to find Marissa and Natalia. And it's probably a solid guess they may be caught up in the middle of this."

As we drove back to Paterson, I stopped for a red light. "Let's take this one step at a time and see what we can find out when we get back to the car wash. Whoever the owner is, they might also have a factory and sell people to businesses like the nail salon."

We drove the rest of the way quietly, not saying much. I'm sure Sam was worrying about her friend, and I was thinking about how much I wanted to call the police right this very second. But if these three women in their blue aprons came from a factory somewhere and if they were already trained workers, why would they be trafficked to a nail salon?

Sam's phone received a message. She clicked it open, and a faint smile broke out on her face for a second. "Wow."

"Some good news?"

"If you could call it that right now. Did I tell you that I'm an actress?"

"No, but it's not like we've had a lot of downtime to learn much about each other," I answered. "Does that smile mean you landed a part?"

"Not yet, but I got a call-back for Monday." She didn't sound enthused, but who could blame her under the circumstances.

"Hey, maybe you and Marissa and Natalia will celebrate together."

She shook her head with a melancholy look on her face. "I really hope so.

CHAPTER NINE

Cruising the streets back to Paterson, I settled down and realized that timing was everything. If we pulled the plug too soon and called the police right now, those on both sides of the business could disappear and we'd never find Marissa and Natalia.

We arrived back where we'd started, and I pulled into a spot where we could still see the car wash but keep out of sight for the most part.

Sam looked at her phone. "Nothing from Marissa. What do we do now?"

"Let's figure this out." I opened the screen to download Snapchat, an app I'd never even heard of, let alone used.

My phone kept asking me for my password, which of course I was always forgetting. I dialed my favorite techxpert who'd set me up with this new phone, my niece Laura.

Sam looked at her phone and then at me. "It's really making me nervous that we haven't heard anything."

As Laura answered my call, I put my finger up to

indicate to Sam that I'd be right with her.

"Hi Laura, it's your Aunt—"

"Hi Aunt Ronnie, I know it's you. How're you doing?"

I loved hearing her cheery voice. "Great. I didn't expect you to pick up. Sorry to bother you at work. I'll make it quick."

"No hurry," she said. "How can I help?"

"Remember when you got me set up with my new phone?"

"Yes." I could hear the amused tone in her voice, and I smiled, remembering the struggle over trying to use my account from the old first-generation iPad I'd used for work a million years ago.

"I want to download an app, but I'm in the field on a case and I can't access my password. Do you happen to remember it?"

"It's easy, it's *Warrior6591* with a capital W."

"Okay. Thanks, kiddo."

"You're welcome," Laura answered. "See you at Thanksgiving."

We signed off. Laura's reference to Thanksgiving reminded me to text Juliana that I'd be late picking up Warrior. She quickly responded that he was welcome to spend the night.

I went back to downloading Snapchat and saw my username on my phone's screen: RL2007@me.com. I slowed down a moment and typed in my password.

That's when I got it.

I stared down at Sam's fingers scrolling through messages. "What kind of phone does Marissa have?"

"An iPhone," she answered.

I opened the Find My app on my iPhone. "Would you happen to know her username and password?"

"Sure, it's how I use her Netflix account when I'm not at her apartment. She uses the same one for almost everything"

"Username, please?"

"marip@me.com, all lower case."

I typed it and handed her my phone to type in the password.

After several seconds of thinking about it, another icon of a tiny iPhone appeared on the map on my phone. "Look, there she is."

Sam studied my phone closely. "Oh my god, you're right." She stared at me as if she was looking at me for the first time.

The amazement in her voice almost made me laugh. "Come on. Let's go find them."

~~~~~

We followed the map in Find My iPhone…a left here, a right there, straight for five miles, and so on. A half hour later, we were still zigzagging through various side streets and marveling at how rapidly the neighborhoods changed—one moment in a newly renovated stretch of apartments with cool design and clean lines, the next few blocks needing to be rebuilt and cleaned up. The phone told us to continue, and we kept on driving. The dot on the screen appeared to be a couple more miles away.

We finally arrived at a one-story motel laid out in a horseshoe fashion with parking in the middle. We pulled over to the curb near a 1950s retro sign for the Peter Pan Lodge. There was nothing nostalgic about the building. The long, dull, grey asphalt roof appeared to squash down the off-white cinderblock walls of the motel.

We took a moment to watch from the corner. There was no one around. I took a pair of powerful binoculars from my glove compartment and tried to see through the large window to the check-in office. I couldn't see anyone there and glanced at the time on my watch.

A lone, tired-looking woman with dark auburn hair shot through with grey walked past our SUV. She was too busy juggling three bags of food to notice us, but Sam and I still slid further down in our seats. She made it across the parking lot without dropping anything and walked over to the door of number twenty-three. A *Do Not Disturb* sign hung from the handle. She propped one bag against the door with her hip, knocked, and grabbed the bag before it could fall.

A curtain moved and then the door opened slowly. A wiry old man with black-rimmed glasses came out, shooed the woman in, and hurriedly looked around to see if anyone had noticed them. Satisfied that no one had, he quickly closed the door.

"Do we think they're in there?" Sam asked, not taking her eyes off the door.

"We definitely need to find out," I said. "That woman was carrying a lot of food, more than for just two people."

"Why wait?" Sam started to open the SUV's door, but I caught her arm and pulled her back.

"Hold on."

"Let's just bust in," she insisted, "and get Natalia and Marissa out of there before something worse happens to them."

"Like I said, we don't even know if they're there, and if they're not, we'll have blown our cover and never find them. One of the men could be watching right this moment."

"I've got an idea." She opened her door and jumped out.

"Wait," I protested, but she took off. I had no choice but to follow, but kept myself hidden at the corner of the building.

I watched Sam walk along one side of the shabby motel until she came to an unmanned housekeeping cart. With an air of authority, she pushed the noisy cart past several rooms then began to call out. As she got closer to number twenty-three, she passed each door with a soft knock and repeated, "Housekeeping."

Number twenty-one opened, and a woman stuck her head out the door. She noticed the cart. "Oh, we've already had our room cleaned."

"Sorry—"

The woman slammed the door shut. Sam glanced over her shoulder toward me and smiled. She rolled the cart to number twenty-two. "Housekeeping." She sang to herself while she knocked and waited. No one responded. She grabbed a clipboard from the cart and spent a moment looking it over, singing and glancing back toward the curtained window of twenty-one.

She rolled the cart to twenty-three, rapped on the door, and bellowed, "Housekeeping."

The door opened ever so slightly, and Samantha froze. "Sorry, checking to make sure someone cleaned your room earlier."

The old man with the glasses cracked the door open more and peered out. "What do you want?"

"Hi, I'm here to make up your room." I could tell from Sam's body language that she was trying to see into the dark room.

"No!" he answered. "The room is good."

She grabbed a pile of folded clean white towels. "Here, let me bring in more towels." From her profile, I could tell she was using her quirky, gap-toothed smile to her advantage.

Sam moved as if to enter the room, but the man slammed the door in her face. Her head jerked back in surprise. "Oh!"

She grabbed the clipboard and checked items off the page, waiting to see if the man would open the door again or if anyone would look out the window. She leaned in and put her ear close to the door.

All of a sudden, the door swung open and an arm reached out, grabbing Sam and pulling her inside. She disappeared into the darkness of the room and the door slammed shut.

CHAPTER TEN

For a moment, I froze in disbelief. I shook myself back to reality, pulled my phone out, and dialed 911, but I held off hitting send. My fist came up as I reached for the door, ready to pound on it and force it open. Instead, the sound of women's voices inside stopped me. I tried to see through the tattered curtains just as the door swung open.

Sam stuck her head out.

"It's okay, it's okay," she said, almost out of breath. "Don't call the police. Get in here, quick."

I stepped into the dark, dingy motel room. Several people milled about, including the older man with the glasses and the tired-looking woman who was busy opening the bags of food.

I stared at a younger woman with choppy, honey-blonde hair, about the same age as Sam. She sat on a small sofa next to a younger girl with a ginger ponytail, but it was hard to see their faces clearly in the dark room. It had to be Marissa and Natalia Popov. Even though they should have looked scared and tense, their body language appeared relaxed instead.

I did a quick scan of the room. This was no hostage situation. To be on the safe side, I told Sam, "Come on, hurry, let's get them out of here."

"You didn't call the police, did you?" Sam looked down nervously at my fingers still clutching my phone.

"Not yet, but I'm prepared to in case something goes down."

"Definitely don't do that," Sam insisted.

I was still ready for a fight, but I narrowed my eyes at the older couple. "It can't just be these two. Where are the other kidnappers?"

The older couple now looked nervous. They looked away.

Marissa said something to the older woman, whom she addressed by her name. Beatriz nodded, said something to her husband, smiled, and cut the sandwiches in half for the group.

This was the weirdest kidnapping ever, I thought to myself as I turned on the lights. That's when I noticed her swollen face.

"Marissa? I'm Ronnie Lake. I don't mean to hurry things along, but are you being held hostage or not? Because it looks like someone slugged you in the face."

"No." Embarrassed, she covered her nose. "I hit a countertop edge with my nose when I fell. That's all. I may have broken it. I'll get it checked out later."

I also noticed some blood on her clothing, maybe from a bloody nose.

"Are you sure? I saw you get pushed into a van and driven away. That certainly looked like a kidnapping." I shrugged. "So, real or not?"

"When we were in the van, I thought we were being kidnapped, and we *were* taken against our will," Marissa answered. "But no, we're not their hostages. We're here of our own free will."

"When did your status change from hostage to—I'm sorry, what?"

She cut me off. "I speak some Spanish, but the men who broke into my father's apartment didn't know that. I listened to what they were saying so I could figure out when to make our move and get away. But we couldn't, and the next thing you know we were forced into the basement and pushed through the dark underground tunnel. What I'd like to know is how did they find out about our building's secret escape tunnel?"

"Me, too," Sam spoke up.

"Anyway, then we stood around for I don't know how much time with our kidnappers," Marissa continued, "and finally someone opened the door, where we came out of the neighboring tower instead of our own building. Then they forced us into the van. My sister and I were terrified."

"It freaked me out, too, when that van drove away." Sam's usually bad ass voice quivered with emotion.

"You saw that?" Marissa asked.

Sam nodded.

Marissa took a drink from her water bottle. "I

learned a lot during the drive to Paterson and even more once we were here at the motel. First, the men didn't know we were gonna be home when they came back. They were only after their passports and visas, the ones that had been confiscated when they trusted their transporters who brought them into the country. My father owns a lot of businesses, including, I learned today, the car washes where these guys work." She physically wilted. "So now I know he's also into human trafficking. They came to our apartment to get their papers back."

"And to take you and Natalia, too," Sam added.

"They weren't coming for us. They were scared to death when we walked in on them and they just panicked," she answered. "We weren't supposed to be there."

"I forgot my inhaler, so we went back," Natalia piped up. "It's my fault."

Marissa jumped in, "No, it wasn't—"

Natalia wouldn't let her sister finish, but pulled her closer and whispered in her ear.

"Go ahead," Marissa answered, and her sister jumped up, ran into the bathroom, and shut the door behind her.

"Is Natalia okay?" Sam asked her best friend.

"Sure. Look, something's gonna happen tonight. The traffickers always keep the women separate from the men when they work and where they sleep. These families worry all the time about being permanently separated because they've seen it happen here, and the traffickers use that as leverage to control them." Marissa paused a moment and then added, "The men believe some of their family members will be among the women being sent away, and they're sure it's happening tonight. They're desperate."

"Hold it. Let's back up a moment," I continued skeptically. "You arrived in Paterson and told the kidnappers that you wanted to treat them to a hotel room as their hide-out until they could free their wives and other family members?"

Marissa looked at me like I was crazy. "No. They already had this room. I'd have gotten them a much nicer room. I even offered, but they said everybody knew to come here and it was too late for a change because it's all happening tonight."

"How'd they even pay for this room? If they're trafficking victims, it's not like they're collecting a regular paycheck."

"Actually, they do get paid. But almost all of it goes to reimburse the traffickers their 'fees' for transportation to the U.S. and other paperwork. It's like a loan with really terrible interest, so they have to pay that back, too. After those deductions, they each get less than a hundred dollars a month. These four families pooled their money and got this room."

"Okay, that makes sense," I said.

Marissa looked at me for a long moment, puzzled. "I've never heard Sam mention you before."

"We just met this morning."

"This morning?" she asked. I nodded, and she continued. "How'd that happen?"

"We crashed into each other right before you texted Sam for help. I'm a private investigator, and Sam hired me to help her retrieve a bag from your place," I said. "Fortunately, that van had a logo, or we wouldn't have known where to start looking for you."

Sam added, "Ronnie's the one who figured out how to find you. Hey, why did you only send *one* message?"

"I got that Snap to you before they took away my phone," Marissa said. "They wanted to make sure I didn't call the police."

"We didn't Snap back because Ronnie and I thought they were real kidnappers," Sam said. "We didn't want you to get hurt."

"It took a while to get them to believe me, that I wanted to help them," Marissa said. "Finally, they gave back my phone a little while ago and I've been charging it." Her sister returned from the bathroom.

"Sam and I are just happy that you and Natalia are safe."

I turned my attention back to the couple, walked over, and extended my hand. "Hi, I'm Ronnie."

Marissa took over. "This is Beatriz and her husband, Rodrigo Braga. The Bragas came up from Brazil, a country with a corrupt government. Life is hard there, plain and simple. They came here for a better life for their children and not this life of slavery. Rodrigo and their son, Tomás, were part of the group that took Natalia and me this morning."

"Where's the rest of the group?" Sam moved to the sofa to sit close to Natalia. She put her arm protectively around the kid's shoulders.

"They mostly work at these car washes around Paterson," Marissa said. "Rodrigo has a later shift, and Beatriz pretended to be ill—"

Beatriz said something to her husband, and he in turn spoke to Marissa, who listened intently.

"I think she ate something to make herself sick, and then when everyone left for work, she slipped out of the woman's dorm," she translated.

"Where does Beatriz work?" I asked, looking at the Bragas.

Marissa again answered. "The women make clothes at a factory. It's in the same building as their dorm. The guys who snatched us are part of this group here in Paterson who were trafficked into this country illegally, mostly from Central and South America. This includes Rodrigo and Beatriz and their kids."

Beatriz picked up the sandwiches, chips, and drinks and offered them around the room. Sam and I both said no thank you but accepted the bottles of water.

Then, as if Marissa had just remembered, she asked Sam, "Did you bring the bag?"

Sam nodded.

"It's inside my tote." I threw her the keys. "Don't forget to lock it."

She opened the door a crack and checked outside. "Be right back." She shut it carefully behind her.

Beatriz ate her sandwich slowly, and Rodrigo wiped his glasses thoroughly before getting up from his chair to check the parking lot from the edge of the curtains in the window.

"I want to help get them away from my dad," Marissa said, "and stay in the U.S."

Sam came inside holding up the navy messenger bag. "Here it is!"

"Are those their documents?" I asked, as Sam handed the bag to Marissa.

"No, it's something better." Marissa looked inside and flipped through the bag's contents.

"What could be better?" Sam asked.

Marissa pulled out a thumb drive. "Everything in this bag will give me leverage to protect this group from deportation. We can do it, in exchange for giving the authorities this evidence against my father."

"Evidence against your father?" Sam asked, incredulous.

"That shouldn't be a surprise. You've heard me complain before. I've known for a long time that he's into some bad stuff. But this human trafficking...like I said, until today I didn't know about that."

"It's too bad the victims don't report the traffickers to the police," Sam said.

I spoke up. "In many cases, they've had bad experiences back in their own countries and they're afraid of the police." I was no expert, but I'd followed a few of these stories in the news.

Marissa continued. "I just don't want them to get deported by ICE after everything they've suffered because of my dad."

"How will you guarantee that the victims don't get kicked out of the country?" I asked. "Do you know anyone who can help?"

Marissa turned to me. "Not yet. I'm kind of hoping you might."

CHAPTER ELEVEN

"I might what?" Puzzled, I wondered where she was going with this.

"Do you have any good contacts in law enforcement?" She pulled a few papers out of the messenger bag and waved them and the thumb drive at me. "I've collected a lot of paperwork that outlines many of my father's crooked businesses all over the world. Plus, there's plenty of other damning evidence about him, like signed agreements and bank accounts." She stuck the papers back in her bag and the thumb drive deep in her hip pocket. "It should be straightforward to make a case and freeze his accounts, and I'll make a trade. My dad in exchange for the safety of these trafficking victims who've been working at his car washes and factory here in Paterson."

I simply stared at her. I knew she was right. Maxim Popov was known as an oligarch who had built a shady fortune, and his global exploits were often featured in the press. That he was still running around free instead of rotting in prison didn't surprise me. The pay-offs must have been huge. But Maxim was Marissa's father, and wouldn't their family bond trump a crime, no matter her father's flaws? I did wonder what exactly had brought her to the point where she was willing to trade him to protect a group of strangers.

I was already thinking about reaching out to my friend Will Benson, who was also my professional mentor, but first I needed to know more. Will took on every kind of case—missing persons, marital disputes and infidelity surveillance, financial fraud investigations, to name a few—and he had a stellar reputation. I'd definitely learned from the best.

At that moment, there was a soft knock on the door. Rodrigo stepped over to the window and peeked out. He looked at Beatriz and Marissa. He spoke in Spanish, but I heard the names "José and Tomás."

"You'll meet the Braga's son," Marissa told us.

As the two men came through the door, I had to stifle my desire to flinch when José, still with the backward ball cap, instead of the hardhat at the tower, entered the room. For a split second I worried he might recognize me from our altercation and my escape from the Popov kitchen. Rodrigo's son, Tomás, still in his black hoodie and olive knit cap, was the young guy who had been there with José searching for their papers. Neither of them had actually seen me, but Sam and I looked at each other across the room and kept quiet.

They seemed surprised to see two of us. Marissa explained in Spanish, with Rodrigo translating into Portuguese, that we were now a team of two and introduced us to Tomás Braga and José Garcia.

"We don't stay long," José said. "Time for a very short lunch. Or the boss will look for us."

The two men sat in chairs near Tomás's parents and began speaking to them. While he talked, I gave Sam money and instructed her to run to a bodega nearby and pick up more ready-made sandwiches and drinks for the two men.

Tomás continued in Portuguese, almost hyperventilating as he spoke to his parents, and then switched to English. "It's maybe ten o'clock. How do we stop them?"

"Tomás, please slow down," Marissa said. She looked at José, too. "Describe exactly what is supposed to happen at ten o'clock?"

José pulled off his ball cap and almost twisted it with a nervous energy. "They will sell some of our women and take them away."

"Take them away where? And for what?"

Tomás jumped in. "We dunno who or why—"

"We dunno where they go. We dunno what they do." José was also speaking faster and faster.

"And where is this happening at ten o'clock?" Marissa asked.

"Maybe at the car wash, maybe at the factory," José answered.

I pulled a chair opposite José. "Please slow down. We want to help. How many are you?"

"Sometimes we are twenty men who work at the car washes, sometimes we are more. Right now, I think twenty. More with the bosses."

"How do you know it's happening at ten tonight?" I asked.

"Because tomorrow ICE comes for an inspection," José answered. "The bosses make everything look good fast before ICE comes."

"Where is Manuel?" Marissa asked. As an aside to me, she mentioned that Manuel had been with José and Tomás and Rodrigo at the apartment this morning.

José responded. "He is at a car wash far from here. Where I work is closer."

"Do you have a wife, mother, sister, or friend who also works for the boss?" I asked. He nodded. "And you're worried she will be taken away?"

"Yes, I worry." José twisted his cap again. "I must get her from the factory." He stood up, determined.

"Wait. Please." I indicated he should sit. "Who is she?"

His voice was ragged by this point and his eyes were watering while he blinked back fast. "My wife, Carolina." He stood up again. "I'll go find her."

"No, José. The boss knows you. But he doesn't know me. I can look for her." I kept my voice calm and reassuring. "What does she look like? Do you have a picture?"

"Not on this phone." He pulled out a flip phone. "The boss gives us this to text us orders. Keep control."

"Tell me what Carolina looks like."

"She's like me. Not a child. We are forty-three. She

works in the factory, and sleeps and eats there. She has hair like mine. Short." He ran his fingers through his dark brown hair. Then he made a two-inch space with his thumb and index finger and placed them on the top right side of his forehead and swept his fingers back. "Grey."

A door opened and Sam walked in with the food.

"She has a grey streak in her short, dark hair?" I asked.

Marissa translated. José nodded in agreement. "Grey streak," he repeated. "When she was twenty-five, she gets a grey streak in her hair. Just there." He again gestured to the top of his head, sweeping his fingers back through his hair. "She always wants to look nice at home and here." He smiled and looked down. "She wears dresses. Not jeans."

"Where's home?

"We traveled from Colombia. Santa Marta. Too many drugs there."

Sam placed the sandwiches and drinks on the table near the two men. "Ronnie and I saw your wife. Just a little while ago."

José's head shot up to look at Sam and then at me. "Where did you see her?"

"A van took her and two teenaged girls to a nail salon." I thought about how that van had passed right by him at the car wash earlier and that he had no idea. "We followed the van, and we know where the salon is. She's not far away." I showed him pictures on my phone of the salon and street signs. I gave him one of the business cards. "Here's the address. Shall I call the police?"

"No police," he snapped, but he had a yearning on his face as if he wanted to say, *Yes, call the police. Right now. Please.*

"Not yet," Marissa instructed. "That'll tip off the traffickers and we won't find the others."

José nodded in agreement. "If you say she is safe, then I'll wait. No police." I could hear the relief in his voice as he rubbed the peppered scruff on his chin.

For all I knew, José may have had negative interactions with the police in Colombia and just assumed it would be the same here in the U.S.

"I think she's safe for the moment," I answered. "How many women work and live at the factory?"

Tomás spoke up this time. "Maybe twenty at the factory. But six or maybe eight, oh, I don't know how many, but the bosses will sell them. My mother works at the factory, but our families..." He gestured around the room. "...we leave tonight, so she stays here, safe. But my sister. We don't know where to find my sister."

"Do you have a picture?" I asked. "What's her name? What does she look like?"

"Ana, she is beautiful." Beatriz came to me, holding out a closed locket hanging around her neck. She opened the clasp to the chain and then opened the locket. Inside was a picture of her son Tomás and her daughter Ana. They looked to be fairly recent photographs judging from the one of Tomás.

Sam came close for a look, too. "Wow."

It wasn't just a matter of a mother saying so, but Ana was breathtakingly beautiful. "Oh my, your daughter is lovely." Her hair was pulled back in the picture, and I could see it was the same dark auburn color as her mother's but without the grey. "Where is Ana today?" I asked.

"At the factory this morning," Beatriz answered. "But I can't find her when I leave." Her eyes teared up with worry.

"Tell me anything else I should know about Ana, so if I find her and talk to her, she will come with me."

Tomás spoke up. "Tell her Mammi and Pappi want you to come. That's what we said when we were children."

"Mammi and Pappi. Okay, anything else?"

Beatriz walked across the room with a limp in her left leg. In Portuguese, she told Rodrigo to explain, and he did in Spanish, and Marissa translated that their daughter had a small but permanent limp from a childhood injury.

"Where is the factory?" I asked. "Is it far from here?"

"First you walk to the car wash where I work," José said.

"We're close to your car wash?" He nodded.

José stood up and got the small pad and pen by the phone. He drew a map and explained as Sam and I watched. He was right. We were so close, I was amazed. We'd been driving around a lot, and I'd thought we were much further away.

"If you see a fat man with red hair, be careful. Ivan is one of the bosses," he said. The map looked easy to follow, but the distance from the car wash to the factory didn't appear to be close.

I looked around at the men. "You said the women sleep at the factory?" They nodded in agreement. "Where?"

They all looked at each other, and Beatriz pointed up with her hand. "Clock." She held up six fingers. "Six."

I nodded. "It sounds like the sixth floor. Is it close to a clock?"

Beatriz nodded in agreement.

"Where do all the men sleep?"

They all spoke up at once. I looked at Marissa, who translated. "It's a very old small warehouse not far from the factory. They all sleep in the same big room."

Marissa paused while the men kept on speaking, and then she continued. "There's one bathroom and the plumbing often gets backed up. There's only one shower, and the place is filthy."

"Where do the men eat their meals?"

They all started to speak again, and Marissa jumped in. "Breakfast is brought to them at the car washes, cold coffee and stale doughnuts most of the time. And take-out dinner is brought to them at the warehouse right at curfew." She listened to the men a little more. "So, if you're late, there won't be any left and you're going to be hungry until breakfast the next morning."

"Marissa, you mentioned Manuel from this morning. He's part of this group?" I asked.

"Yes. He found Natalia's inhaler," she said.

"And brought it to me," Natalia added.

I asked the group. "Is Manuel looking for someone, too? Someone at the factory?"

Rodrigo answered. "Yes."

"What can you tell me about her?" I asked.

Beatriz took off in rapid Portuguese and her husband did an almost simultaneous translation into Spanish, and then Marissa put it in English.

"Even though they're cousins, they are really like brother and sister. Close. Went to school together. They're both twenty-five. They came up from Mexico to work and send money to their families. They ended up with a bad coyote and now they're trapped here. They tried three times to leave together. So, the boss had her disappear."

"What's her name?" I asked and pulled out my notecard and pen.

"Yolanda," Beatriz answered.

"What are their last names?" I wrote the names of everyone I'd been meeting in this group—first and last.

"They are both Hernandez," Rodrigo said. "Their fathers are brothers."

"Any pictures?"

Beatriz pulled out her phone and showed me a photo of the two of them standing by a sewing machine.

I noticed it wasn't a flip-phone. "You have a different phone from José?"

"No." She pulled out a flip-phone exactly like the one José showed me and then put it back. Rodrigo spoke and Marissa translated. "Rodrigo, Tomás, and Beatriz bought this other phone together at the bodega with their money. It's for when they run, and then they'll throw away the Boss's phone."

"May I see the picture of Yolanda for a moment?" I gestured for Sam to come close and look, too. Yolanda was a tall, lean young woman with a mop of dark curly unruly hair. She towered over Beatriz. "She's very tall."

"Yes, yes." Beatriz reached up with her hand over her head to show how much taller Yolanda was. She took one final look at the picture of her with Yolanda, and her face settled into sadness.

José gave Tomás a look, and they both stood up. "We go back to work and see you here later," José said. Then he spoke in Spanish to Marissa, and she answered back in Spanish.

Tomás stood by the window, cracked open the curtain, and checked outside. He nodded at José that the coast was clear, and they left.

After a few moments, Sam spoke up. "What do we do now? Take this trafficking ring down?"

"First, I have to make a call to get a deal going to protect the victims once the authorities move against the traffickers. Marissa, you protect that messenger bag and thumb drive. The feds will need it to make any charges against your dad stick."

For the next fifteen minutes, she did show me a few documents and accounts. I knew I shouldn't be shocked, but it was certainly an eye-opener to realize how much more sordid Maxim Popov's business interests were than what had generally been portrayed in the press. This oligarch should not have been running around free, let alone living up in the Manhattan clouds in his luxurious tower apartment. A deep, dark hole in the ground to bury him alive would still be too good for this animal.

CHAPTER TWELVE

Will Benson had brought me into this profession, and I'd always be indebted to him for it. We'd originally met at the Aikido dojo where we both practiced—he was a third-degree black belt, and I was also a black belt, but first-degree. At the time, I'd hired him to look into a case concerning my brother.

In the beginning, Will had taken me under his wing as a sort of intern, and I'd helped him work on cases while I went to school and got my license. Once certified, I'd begun doing more and more cases solo, and my new business as a private eye took off.

At the moment though, I had to listen to Will almost lose it over the phone when he found out my target was the notorious Maxim Popov.

He warned me that getting involved in any case that concerned Popov could have fatal consequences. Of course, he wanted to know how I got so lucky as to land this case, and when I told him I'd more or less accidentally stumbled into it, he hung up on me.

Will called me back in less than thirty seconds.

"Before I go out on a limb and burn up a few favors—including with a very pretty immigration attorney who might not want to go out with me again after this—are you sure this is for real?" Will asked with his tell-tale, inherent skepticism.

"I've seen some of the documents that she has in her bag. It's all pretty horrifying."

"You said it's all coming to a head tonight. I can drop everything to help," he offered, although I couldn't help but wonder if the offer was just a way to make sure I stayed out of danger.

"I have to be careful to not jump the gun before we find those women. If the traffickers get wind of any police, they'll disappear and take the rest of their victims with them."

"I'll work on getting a written agreement. Do you have any idea how many victims we're talking about?" Will asked.

"From what I've heard from some of the workers, it could be almost fifty." I could hear him exhale slowly.

"Okay. Let me get to work on it. Let's check back later." Will hung up.

Sam and I stood near the door to the motel room with Marissa.

"Let's go," Sam said. "I'll head to the factory to find the other women—"

"Hold it." I stopped her. "One of us has to stay here to wait with Marissa and see if anyone else comes by with new information, say, an update on tonight—"

"Okay—"

"And that's *your* job, Sam." I tried to look reassuring, then added, "Come to think of it, I do have something else for you to do. Tell you more in a moment." Then I switched my attention to Marissa.

"I need you to think of one of your father's good friends or a family member, somebody whose name I can drop that's meaningful to his men just in case I get into a jam."

"That's easy," she answered. "Anybody who works with my dad knows that Alex Ivanov is his right-hand guy."

I repeated his name slowly. Marissa nodded.

I pulled out the map that José had drawn to get to the factory. "Alex Ivanov, that's not the fat man with the red hair that José warned us about?"

"No."

"Wait, that was Ivan, wasn't it? Not Ivanov."

Marissa shrugged. "I don't know who that Ivan is."

"Okay. I've got it straight," I said to her. Turning to Sam, I continued. "I've got a couple of things to get ready for surveillance. Give me a few minutes and then come out to my car. You can help me get set up."

"I'll be out in a sec." She hurried into the bathroom.

I used my head start to quickly change inside my SUV into jeans, boots, jacket, and a warm scarf. I stuffed some cash into my jeans pocket and also dug out a credit card and ID that I duct-taped to my leg above my ankle. I pulled my thick sock up and pushed my foot back into the boot. Then I walked a couple of steps to make sure nothing was rubbing.

Next, I grabbed a vehicle tracker and a baseball cap with a built-in tracker and checked them on their apps on my phone. I glanced at my FitBit and checked it, too. You never knew when these sorts of tools would come in handy. Then I hid my own tote with the Louis Vuitton duffle in the bottom of a big canvas zipper bag that I locked and covered with extreme weather clothing. Finally, I squished the pile behind an empty ice chest and Sam's bike in the back of my SUV.

I opened another bag and pulled out a few items, including a small black plastic box, and Sam appeared. "What's up?" she asked.

"I'm taking some gear with me and I want you to know what tools I've got." I slid open the clunky heel on my boots. I held up a small plastic two-inch by one-inch box. "This is a GPS tracker." I turned it on and pointed at another button. "This is a panic button, if I get into trouble."

"How will I know if you hit the button?" she asked.

I put my hand out. "Give me your phone."

She looked at me in surprise but placed it in my palm. I downloaded the app and showed her its features and how to check it for my location or a panic button notification.

"This is a backup tool I like to have on me in case I disappear and my phone is taken from me. You'll always know where I am. If there's any kind of trouble, please call this friend of mine." I typed in Will Benson's cell number. "Only call him if it's a dire emergency. Got it?"

"I promise. Anything else I need to know?"

"Remember, my phone will also work as a GPS tracker. But if for some reason I'm separated from my phone, the tracker in my boot heel should work just fine."

"Any other tricks of the trade?" Sam asked snarkily, the beginning of a smile playing around her mouth.

"This isn't a joke," I snapped, and she stepped back slightly. "It's not some lame thriller action movie. These are nasty, deadly people we're dealing with. If you can't handle this, please speak up so I'll know I won't rely on you in case things go badly. Whatever you decide is okay."

She looked down at her hands, somewhat chastened. "I didn't mean to joke. You can count on me."

"Since Marissa wants to protect everyone who's been trafficked, I think we should start to gather pictures so that she's got some way of defining the actual group when she makes the trade for her father."

"How do we do that without freaking out everyone when they see a phone come out to take their pictures?" She pretended to snap a shot of me with her phone. "Seeing someone do that would send me for the hills."

I reached into the gear bag and pulled out a pair of sunglasses. "Wear these. While I go check out the factory, I think you should use my car and go back to all the Popov car washes, this time to vacuum the car interior, and photograph all the men working at each location. Once I've got you set up, which will only take a sec, all you need to do when you want a shot is look in their direction, reach up, and press this button on the glasses."

"What are you going to use at the factory?" She tried them on. "Do you have a second pair?"

I pulled out a different small gadget from my bag and threaded it through one of the button holes on my jacket. "If I can get inside the factory, I'll use this button camera. It's very discreet."

"You actually get decent pictures with that little thing?" Sam looked skeptical as she peered closely at the round button on the front of my jacket.

"They're just fine." I smiled and slipped the camera's small remote into my pocket. "Sam, you should hurry. It's already close to five, and we're losing light fast. When you're finished taking pictures at the car washes, we'll keep my car at the motel. It's easier to park here, and it's out of the way. No one will notice it." I tossed her the keys. "Keep it locked."

Sam nodded, folded the glasses, and put them in her pocket.

"Please tell Marissa what's going on, and I'll be back in a couple of hours." I started walking and slid the ball cap inside my jacket.

~~~~~

I arrived at the car wash to find José on the sidewalk arguing with a red-haired fat man. It had to be Ivan. It was all in Spanish, and I couldn't understand any of it. The body language was pretty clear when Ivan shook his fist in José's face, though, emphasizing his point with a menacing tone of voice. José caught the man's fist and said something back to him.

Ivan wheeled around and took off. José, who had spotted me, gave me an oh-so-slight nod to follow the fat man. I stuck José's map in my pocket.

I did my best to keep other people on the sidewalk between Ivan and me. I had no idea where we were going. I kept up, maintaining enough of a distance that I hoped he wouldn't spot me.

He turned onto South Main Street, and I could see we were in a Middle Eastern neighborhood because of the signs. It was an obvious tip-off when unfamiliar business names were followed by 'Authentic Turkish Cuisine' or 'Syrian Bakery.' I noticed a lot of takeout, butchers, bakeries, cafés, and restaurants that lined the busy streets, and I remembered somewhere I'd heard that Paterson is a foodie's paradise. Toros Takeout looked so inviting that I made a mental note as I dashed by to come back and visit the next chance I had.

The man was moving faster now, and I rushed to keep up. Ivan was definitely huffing and puffing, and I even got close enough to hear him wheezing at one point.

Several blocks later when we crossed 21st Avenue, we arrived at another neighborhood, also vibrant and filled with people. A sign said "Colombian Corridor," and many of the names on restaurants, coffee shops, bodegas, bars, and stores were now in Spanish.

It was dusk, and the street lights and most of the store lighting were already on. The neighborhood had a wonderful, pulsating energy. I heard Spanish being spoken all around as people passed by. I could also have easily been distracted here—there was so much to see—but I worried I'd lose sight of Ivan.

He screeched to a halt and dashed into a small coffee bar. I stopped in front of a shop across the street where I inhaled the aroma wafting from the bar as I stared into the window at rows of shoes, watching in the reflection for when he'd exit. My nose twitched—what else was I smelling? Toasted pistachios and garlic. Five minutes later, he came out, sipping from a small plastic cup. He stood for a moment enjoying his espresso then tossed the cup into a recycle bin, and off he went again.

We continued on Main Street, heading north into the heart of the busy downtown that bustled with traffic and pedestrians. I passed by two massive, beautiful historic buildings, one with a lovely old dome and the other a tower.

I dashed on, my eyes sweeping inside lobbies and down side streets when I realized I'd lost Ivan in a crowd of people. I got a knot in my stomach before getting a glimpse of his red hair a block-and-a-half ahead of me and rushed to catch up.

We made our way through another of Paterson's historic districts, this one industrial with enormous nineteenth century mills, factories, and machine works.

I crossed McBride Avenue and could see Ivan was getting further ahead of me again. I arrived at the Passaic River, only to be stunned by the sight of a gigantic waterfall cascading over craggy rocks. I'd seen photographs, but in person it was a much more powerful sight. I did a double-take when Ivan hoofed it across a wrought-iron footbridge over the falls, the early twilight sky above him.

I hurried to the bridge and started running across on its ancient wooden boards. Looking down at my feet did nothing to tamp down my worry that the entire structure would break apart and come crashing down.

Pull it together, Ronnie. You're being ridiculous. Of course, this is a sturdy footbridge. I tried my best to keep my eyes on Ivan and not allow my gaze to drift down at the roaring water below.

The noise of the traffic receded as the thundering sound of the crashing water took over. I could feel the spray from the foaming water that hit the rocks. My boots glistened with droplets of water. Exposed heights were not my thing, and I suddenly felt lightheaded. I stopped, grabbed onto the railing, inhaled deeply, and exhaled slowly. My head cleared and I looked around.

Ivan was already off the bridge and heading for a rundown stadium. Next thing I knew, he was gone. He'd stepped into some trees and just disappeared.

I kept my eyes locked on the spot as I ran off the bridge, down the path, and toward the sign for the Hinchcliffe

Stadium. At one time, it must have been really grand, but not now, and all the graffiti certainly didn't help. I ran to the spot in the trees where I'd last seen Ivan.

There was a hole in the fence, and I stepped into the darkness cast by the branches of the trees. I climbed up a bank and stared out at a stadium filled with bleachers that were overrun by trees and shrubs. Ivan was walking across an enormous athletic field.

I didn't want him to spot me in this wide-open space, so I gave Ivan time to cross and leave the field. Then I dashed over to the other side.

As I came out on the street, Ivan was walking under a dark overpass. The low light made everything eerie, and I once again wondered how I'd gotten myself into this mess.

I had to do my best to see this through. I looked in every direction in the shadows as I walked beneath the overpass.

There was more light on the other side where I saw a huge old factory. Its dark brick exterior was massive, topped by a sturdy clock tower. I counted six floors—that was nothing in Manhattan but definitely tall in Paterson.

I stood out of sight. Ivan casually walked down a side street at the same time that a medium-sized truck drove up and stopped just beyond the door. He checked in with a man holding a clipboard, who straightened up quickly when he saw him. They spoke to each other, the man checked the sheet on his clipboard, and then the two of them walked inside through colossal doors.

CHAPTER THIRTEEN

-Have you found any of the women?

Sam was certainly impatient. I texted back.

-Not yet. Have arrived at factory.

-What's it like?

-Old clock tower building. Will txt later.

It was close to five o'clock, and I still had a lot to find out before the 10 pm deadline. There was still business activity here, as several small vans pull up behind the truck at the door and the racks of clothing. I walked over, thinking the vehicles wouldn't be easily noticed on this side street. The scene reminded me of the garment district in Manhattan.

I crossed the street and pretended to be a passerby, excited by a rack of cute skirts. I handled the skirts on their hangers and ran my fingers over the fabric, admiring and appraising but really trying to find the designer or manufacturer's tag.

"Oooh, these are cute," I cooed. The man pushing the rack looked scared. "Can I buy one? In there?"

The man mumbled in a shaky voice, "No. This is a factory."

"Oooh, a factory outlet," I headed for the door. "Can I go in and shop—"

"No." A big burly man out of nowhere cut me off. "No store here, lady," he said in broken English with an unidentifiable accent.

"Where can I buy them?" I tried to look at the tag hanging from the skirt. "Ah, I don't know this designer." Several men came out of the building carrying large cardboard boxes that they loaded into the truck.

The boss blocked my way and kept me from the skirt racks. "Lady, get out of here."

I looked at him as if I couldn't believe what he was saying to me. "Don't you know who I am?" My tone was overly indignant as I glanced around. Another van arrived and workers continued quickly loading clothes. They all looked terrified.

The guy pushing the skirt rack stumbled and the stand tipped over, scattering hangered skirts all over on the sidewalk.

I reached my hand out to help him. "Are you okay?" His hand was bloody from having scraped his palm on the rough surface of the sidewalk.

Blood dripped on a couple of the skirts, and the boss went ballistic. "You worthless piece of shit," he screamed at the worker.

I tried again with the man who fell down. "Here, let me help you."

As I leaned over extending my hand again, the big man grabbed my other arm.

"Don't you dare touch me." I stood my ground, hanging on tightly to my tote. "I'm a friend of the Popov family, specifically Alex Ivanov."

And that's when I saw it—the flash of fear in the big man's eyes. It was there one moment and then gone the next. I knew I'd struck a nerve.

"Alex Ivanov," the man repeated slowly. He had let go of me, but he didn't move.

I made a quick decision to up the ante. "Kate Popov always told me—"

"You saw her?" he interrupted and took my arm again. "When?"

I shook loose. "Hey, what's the big deal? It was just the other day." I continued to play along. "Why? When was the last time you saw her?"

He didn't say a word and just stared at me for a very long moment.

"I came by for one thing," I said over my shoulder as I looked around. "To buy some skirts, and Alex and then Kate told me I could find good ones here at the factory."

He waved toward the door. "I will take you to the showroom." He hurried me inside and rushed me down a long hallway.

"What is going on here? I just wanted to buy skirts."

More boxes lined the hallway, and I was getting a bad feeling about this.

He opened a door and stepped into a dark room. "Follow me."

That was about the time I wanted to run, but he flipped on the lights. I tried to slow my breathing as I looked around at all the merchandise, the racks of skirts and dresses.

"Please, you are our guest. Take your time." He left, and I was surprised to find myself in the middle of a small show room in this ugly, squat building, looking at some perfectly lovely clothing.

This was all so peculiar. I felt like Alice falling down the rabbit hole as the day continued to get more and more bizarre.

The door opened and the supervisor entered, the one who had earlier walked into the building with Ivan. I was surprised to find the man apologetic about the confrontation in front of the building and appreciative that I'd stepped in. I wasn't buying any of this, but I'd play along to see where this was going. He introduced himself as Boris.

"I understand you'd like to buy skirts?" Boris asked. "Cash is best."

"No problem," I answered. "My daughters and I are all a size six. I've got two hundred dollars for skirts. These are the ones, if you still have them in our size." I circled the room, pointing out a half-dozen different styles. The man pulled out a small pad and pen and took notes.

"Give me five minutes to see what I have. I'll be back soon with skirts." And he left.

I looked around and noticed three other doors in this show room. The first one I tried was a small restroom; the second opened into a supply cabinet where I found a large pair of scissors that could come in handy as a weapon if I needed one; and the third was locked. But the lock felt loose and the door jiggled. I put my ear up, and all was quiet on the other side.

I pushed at the door. It almost opened, but not quite. I jiggled the knob again, and this time it worked.

I stepped into another office, but this one had a large window on the wall opposite the door. I hurried over and looked down at a modest-sized room lit by fluorescent lights. There must have been almost twenty women of all ages scattered around the space. They all wore blue work aprons with pockets for their sewing tools. Now I knew the three women delivered to the nail salon had come from this factory.

On one side, a smaller group, maybe a half dozen, were busy unrolling bolts and cutting fabric. Sewing machine stations filled the rest of the space, and behind each one sat a woman focused on running material through her machine to stitch together a skirt or a dress. Besides the machine, each sewer was surrounded by work tables to lay out fabric and garments. Scissors, tape measures, and boxes filled with spools of different colored threads also lay scattered across the work surfaces.

Two male managers patrolled the floor, watching all the women and checking their work product. Sometimes one of them stopped a worker behind a machine to demand a correction. Even though I couldn't hear a word through the window, I could see in the body language down on the floor that it was a dictatorial workplace.

One young girl raised her hand, and one of the managers came over to her station. I could see her ask him something. He looked annoyed as he glanced at his watch but then nodded for her to accompany him. As they crossed the room, the girl made eye contact with a woman in her mid-thirties. The woman looked worried. He took the girl to a door that he unlocked, and they went through. The door closed behind them.

Meanwhile, the other manager scolded an older woman who must have made a mistake cutting fabric. She sat stiff as a statue, looking straight ahead, absorbing the verbal abuse.

Less than five minutes later, the other guy returned with the teenager. As she walked back to her station, I saw the thirty-something woman again make quiet eye-contact with her. An idea was forming in my mind.

My eyes swept over the entire room, carefully looking at each face, trying to determine if any of them were related to the men I'd met at the motel. I knew that José's wife Carolina was at the nail salon Sam and I had visited earlier. I knew that Manuel's cousin Yolanda was missing and probably wouldn't be here. I looked carefully for Tomás's sister, Ana, but couldn't spot her.

I was running out of time and needed to get over to the showroom before the supervisor returned. In looking back and forth between the door to the showroom and the factory floor, I almost missed her. In the far-left corner, a sewer got up from her machine with her finished item of clothing. As she walked over to another seamstress, I caught the slight limp. I froze in order to watch. It was less of a limp than her mother had shown me at the motel. When she held up the dress, she lifted her face, but I couldn't see her closely.

I quickly slipped back through the door, landed on the chair, rummaged through my tote, and crossed my legs just as the supervisor came into the showroom. Both of his arms were up in the air holding hangers as he managed to bring over many more than the six skirts I'd requested. I paid cash for the original six and added one more to the pile to reward him for his extra efforts.

"Now, let's get down to why I'm really here and the business I'd like to do with you." He looked at me very suspiciously. "Relax. As I told you, I'm friends with the Popovs and Mr. Ivanov. "

"Yes," he said.

"A year ago, my husband surprised me with a new housekeeper for my birthday. He arranged everything directly with Maxim." I hemmed and hawed uncomfortably.

"Go on," he said. I could tell I had his attention.

"It was great until about three months ago." I folded

my hands in my lap and looked down as if I was struggling to come up with the right words.

"What happened?"

"She started screwing my husband."

"Your housekeeper?" He said it like he couldn't believe it.

"She was very young and pretty." I looked him straight in the eye. "I got rid of her."

He looked at me in shock at the thought that I'd done something extreme.

"No, no," I insisted. "I didn't kill her. I sent her to work at my sister's place."

"So how can I help you?"

"It's really very simple," I answered. "I don't want my husband surprising me with another beautiful, young housekeeper. I want to do the choosing this time."

Boris looked genuinely surprised. He chuckled.

"What's so funny?" I looked at him matter-of-factly.

"I never have the wife come and ask to choose for the husband." He looked generally bewildered.

"Well, there's a first time for everything." I pulled more bills out of my pocket. "My husband pays Mr. Popov directly, but I have this." I peeled off five one-hundred-dollar bills. "You could take your wife out for a very nice dinner."

Boris gave me another slow smile as he took the bills from me. "Follow me."

We walked through what was no longer a mystery

door for me into the neighboring office, and he walked me over to the large window. We looked out over the modest factory floor.

His arm swept the window's expanse. "We can make arrangements for any of these women to be your housekeeper."

"But aren't these women the seamstresses who make your clothes? What will you do without them?"

"We have new women coming soon," he said. "So some of these ladies are free to go to new jobs. And prices are good, too."

"Wait a minute. Some of these women are too pretty," I noted.

"Yeah, which ones?" he asked.

"Those two." I pointed at two early twenty-something women with lovely features and long, dark wavy hair.

"Sisters from Honduras," he answered. "They are very good seamstresses. Their father was a tailor back home."

"And look at that one in the corner with the reddish hair." I gestured toward Tomás's sister. "Way too pretty."

"Yeah, but she don't walk right," Boris said.

"What do you mean?" I asked, knowing full well what he meant.

He impersonated her limp.

"Hmm. I wish I could see better."

"Come on. Follow me." He opened another door to

a back stairway and we walked down the narrow steps and out onto the small factory floor. That was when the heat assaulted me. It didn't take long for me to feel sticky from my own perspiration. I noticed some of the women had beads of sweat running down their faces, which they wiped off with their forearms, trying their best not to drip on the clothing they were sewing. The ventilation was poor, and there was no air circulation. Did these women ever pass out from the heat in here?

Long fluorescent tubes hung from the ceiling to light the space. A few flashed and needed changing. The walls were the same dark brick of the exterior. The floor was a dirty linoleum, cracked in places, peeling in others.

The women looked at me curiously for a moment, glanced at Boris, and squinted back down at their work. It seemed that none of them wanted to draw attention to herself. Some of the older women looked exhausted, with deep circles under their eyes. Their shifts were probably very long, early starts with few breaks until they ended maybe twelve or sixteen hours later.

"You can choose any lady and take her with you," Boris said. "I will call Maxim to let him know. I'm sure he will say it is okay."

"No, no," I insisted, even though I wanted to take all of them with me out of here. "My husband will be angry if he finds out I came here to choose one of your workers." I gave Boris a conspiratorial smile. "Here's what I need you to do." And I explained to him that I'd choose four or five here, and that when my husband would come by, Boris would only show him those five, and not the ones who were too young and pretty.

We walked up and down the aisles, and I tried to slow things down and pause a nano-second to smile and make eye contact with each seamstress or the women cutting the fabric and secretly snap a picture. This made Boris nervous, as he tried to hurry me along.

We came to the sisters from Honduras. Up close I could see they were in their teens, not their twenties.

"Hello," I said coldly for Boris' benefit, snapping their pictures discreetly when they looked up at me.

They looked confused for a moment until they felt Boris's gaze and then immediately dropped their eyes to look at their work again. I was struck by their youth. One looked fourteen and the other couldn't have been more than fifteen or sixteen. They were still children, for God's sake.

We continued walking around, and every now and then I'd signal to Boris a candidate for him to show my so-called husband in choosing a new housekeeper. As we made our way down the last aisle and toward Tomás's sister, a phone rang on the other side of the factory. Boris waved me on to continue looking while he walked away to answer the phone.

I took a couple more pictures as I walked in Ana's direction. I don't know what made me do it, but I quickly unsnapped my FitBit tracker from my wrist, slipped it in my pocket, and walked up to Ana. "Hi, how are you?" I patted my tote with my other hand, feeling the ball cap with the built-in tracker.

She looked up from her sewing machine, and I secretly snapped a picture. "I am fine," she said, shyly looking back at her work. "Thank you." I could definitely report back to Beatriz that her daughter was here safe and sound and that she'd not yet been sent somewhere as somebody else's slave.

"What are you working on?" I asked.

"A dress, a beautiful dress." She finished the seam, stood up, and showed it to me, a colorful halter-dress with a carwash-skirt overlay out of a matching chiffon fabric. She shook it a bit, and the carwash strands of fabric swooshed like a flapper dress from the 1920s.

I said very quietly. "I bet your Mami and Papi would admire your excellent work." I discreetly pulled out the FitBit from my jacket pocket and the ball cap from my tote and slid both under some fabric on the table.

Her eyes flashed for only a second, and I winked. Again, I kept my voice very quiet. "They are well, and Tomás, too." I felt the fabric on the dress. "Something will happen later, so be careful. Try to get away and keep my things with you. They will help me find you."

I turned on my heel and walked toward the door just as Boris was heading in my direction. I looked back and waved. "Thank you for showing me that beautiful dress."

Two women, who moments ago had been sewing at

their machines, were now assembling and taping packing boxes. I walked around them, eager to leave.

"Have you decided on any more?" he asked, and I quietly pointed out three more women heading toward middle age that he should show to my supposed husband.

"Thank you for helping me, and Mr. Ivanov will be in touch to make arrangements." We walked up the stairs and through the door back into the office with the window, where I first viewed the factory floor and its women workers. Then we moved back into the show room where I gathered the skirts I'd purchased and put them into a couple of large shopping bags that Boris gave me.

As we walked back down the hallway to the entrance, I thanked him again and said goodbye. It was all I could do to not explode through the doors into the fresh air and take off running as fast as my feet would carry me. The vans were gone, as well as the workers who had been loading the racks of clothing. I glanced at the truck, which was now half-filled with boxes. While I was inside, another similar-sized truck had also pulled up in front of it. As I walked by it and looked inside the open doors, I wondered about several cases of water along one of the walls and a pile of blankets stacked in one corner. Something about this scene didn't make sense, and my intuition told me it was important to pay attention.

I dropped one of my bags alongside the truck, my shopping bag's contents spilling on the sidewalk. I leaned over to put the skirts back in the bag and discreetly slapped my GPS tracker underneath the truck. I stood up and twirled around as I repositioned both bags on each shoulder, checking to see if anybody had seen me placing the tracker. I didn't spot anyone or any cameras.

Still, I walked away quickly. I crossed the street in the direction of the overpass and wondered if I'd made a bad decision leaving Ana in there.

I looked back and up at the top floors of the factory. I counted up to the sixth and viewed the clock tower on top.

As I walked away, I remembered as many faces as I could from the factory floor, even though I had pictures of them all in my hidden camera. Most of them had probably come from south of the border to seek a better life. Unfortunately, they'd been trapped into slave labor instead.

I'd heard and read accounts about how pervasive this was here. How many other sweat shops like this were there across the country, filled with somebody's child, somebody's parent, all with a tale of hardship? I'd just looked into the eyes of about twenty or so of those heartbreaking stories.

I couldn't save every victim in the country, and I couldn't put a stop to this horror. But I could do something about those women I'd just seen.

CHAPTER FOURTEEN

It was almost dark outside, and instead of walking back to the motel with my shopping bags full of skirts, I asked Sam to pick me up. I continued watching the activity around the two trucks—more boxes went into one and several piles of sweaters into the other. Fortunately, bright lights around the entrance made it easier to conduct my surveillance.

Sam texted back that she'd finished driving to all the car washes to take pictures of the men. All had gone well, except José had been surprised to see her pull up to the fifth one. Fortunately, he stayed cool and didn't give her away.

Sam was now back at the motel with Marissa and Natalia, and she'd even taken pictures of everyone there. All was quiet for the moment.

As I sat on steps in a dark doorway and waited, I watched a big black shiny Mercedes pull up. Boris and Ivan ran out as a glamorous but brassy, tough-looking blonde got out of the car, clicking the lock button on her fob.

This wasn't a retail clothing store, nor the kind of place where you expected a high-end shopper to come. And this lady looked like she knew how to shop, a real pro. I pulled my binoculars from my bag and took a closer look. She was wearing the latest in fashion, and even at this distance, I was able to see her shoes and bag were expensive.

She was clearly some kind of big shot, treating Boris and Ivan as if they were her servants. But they accepted her disdain and followed her inside, leaving her car unattended.

I switched my focus back to the top floors just beneath the clock tower, wishing I could check out the women's dorm. I wondered what their quarters looked like.

I put my field glasses down and continued watching the enormous double doors, expecting this uber-shopper-woman to exit, but nothing happened. Sam arrived, and I quickly made my way to the SUV. She took the passenger seat and I slid in on the driver's side, tossing my bags in the back.

Boris and Ivan came outside for a smoke break and talked.

"What do we do now?" Sam asked, her foot tapping nervously.

"Let's stay put for a moment and see if anything interesting happens," I responded.

One of the men got a text and said something to the other one, and then both of them looked inside the door.

Boris rushed over to the Mercedes with the fob, unlocked it, and started the car. He walked back to the entrance of the factory.

All of a sudden, the two men jumped to attention and Ivan pulled the big heavy double door open. The brassy woman swept through, and Boris rushed to open the driver's side door. Another man dressed in shirt sleeves with the cuffs rolled up exited the building and followed the woman.

As they stepped closer to the car, he pulled her into a huge embrace They kissed each other deeply. Boris and Ivan looked at each other knowingly and then looked away.

The man whispered something in the woman's ear, and she threw her head back and laughed. He kissed her on the neck and she laughed again.

They both walked around the car, and she slowed down so that her hips swung from side to side and he could admire her from the back. She turned around, gave him a look, blew a kiss, then got in the car.

Sam and I just looked at each other. "Can you believe this?" she sneered.

The woman revved the engine and shot away from the factory, then quickly slowed down to a more normal speed.

"Let's follow that Mercedes." I pulled away from the curb as all three men went inside the clock tower.

"Where do you think we're going this time?" Sam asked, as I drove after the Mercedes.

"That may have been the man in charge of that factory and his very sexy wife." At the moment it was easy to keep enough distance and still follow the sedan. "So no, I don't know where we're heading. It's all part of—"

Sam finished my sentence. "Being a private investigator."

I smiled at her. "Any better ideas?"

"Let's do it," she said. "Whatever we can do to help Marissa and Natalia, and sooner rather than later."

This time our drive took us even further out of town. After about forty minutes, the neighborhoods with lawns got nicer and the houses more expensive. Finally, we pulled into a new development of multi-million-dollar McMansions. Each was more oversized than its neighbor and unique in its architectural style.

The black Mercedes pulled into the driveway of number twenty-one Chateaux Road. The exterior lighting illuminated all the features of a sprawling Italian villa with too much stucco and too many arches. I stopped my car well before the woman's house and across the street for a good view. The door to the attached garage slowly opened.

As the blonde in the Mercedes drove up to park, the massive ornate front door of the villa swung open, and she stopped the car. Two young girls—maybe nine and five—waited quietly at the door in their black tights and school uniforms. A tall, lean young woman with dark, unruly hair, wearing jeans and a long-sleeved white tee-shirt underneath an oversized faded coat, stood behind them. She squatted down in order to speak to them softly and then gently touched their shoulders to encourage them to go. They did as they were told, but not with as much enthusiasm as one would expect from kids happy to see a loving parent. After a moment, the young woman jogged after the kids, but now they were focused on the car and the person in it.

"Wait a minute," I mumbled.

"What?" Sam asked.

"I think that's Manuel's cousin, Yolanda. Beatriz showed us her picture, remember? That curly, wild dark hair? Tall and skinny?"

She took a moment to really look at Yolanda. "Yeah, I think you're right."

The woman got out of the Mercedes and scooped up the girls with hugs and kisses. It was subtle, but I noticed that the girls stiffened ever so slightly during the physical affection showered upon them. The woman cooed over her daughters and then stopped to notice something the matter with the younger girl's tights.

She turned to their nanny and started screaming at her. I watched Yolanda's body take the verbal blows and saw her lanky frame shrink. I couldn't hear the specifics, but it was clear that Yolanda was trying to reason with the woman. It was no use. The tough blonde was out of control, screeching and yelling. The younger daughter stiffened and her chin quivered. I pressed the button and the driver's side window silently opened.

Now I could hear more as the older girl stuck up for

the nanny. "Please mama, it's not so bad. It's not Yolanda's fault."

"Oh Gabriella, my dear, I leave Yolanda in charge," this witch of a mother answered to the older one, "and she's supposed to make sure that everything is perfect for you and your sister. Her job is to take care of you when I can't because I have other important things I need to do for our business." Mama paused dramatically for a moment, staring deeply into each girl's eyes. "And why is that so important, my sweet darlings?"

The girls and their mother said in unison, "Because the work makes much money, which pays for nice things, and makes our lives special." Obviously, this was an oft-repeated catchphrase.

The younger daughter bravely piped up. "I fell inside. It was an accident. Please don't be mad at Yolanda," she begged her mother in a squeaky, childlike voice. Even though I could hear them speaking clearly, I wanted a closer look and discreetly used my binoculars.

"Oh, my precious Arianna." She tightly hugged her little girl, whose expression was one of fear. Her big sister continued to step back, putting more space between herself and her mother. She looked sad, too.

"Come around children and help me with my bags." Their mother opened the trunk of the Mercedes. "I got you each something special." She handed her older daughter a paper bag with a Chanel logo. The girl peeked inside and pulled out a hot-pink mini designer bag, a gift too old for a nine-year-old.

"Thank you, Mama," Gabriella said politely.

Switching focus to her younger daughter, the woman continued. "Arianna, come with me." She almost heaved the child off her feet in her zeal to pull her around to the back door of the sedan. "This is for you, and I'm sure you're going to love it." The woman tugged at something in the back seat, then extricated a hot pink three-wheeler scooter. It was perfect for a five-year-old, like a miniature chic Italian Vespa.

As Arianna pushed the scooter toward the front door, her meek expression transformed into an ear-to-ear smile until both sisters glanced over to Yolanda, who still looked worried. The mother's excitement changed into annoyance until Yolanda stepped up, put a smile on her face, and said pleasantly, "Madame, I will try harder. Please let me help you with your bags."

She reached inside the trunk and pulled out two brightly colored shopping bags with famous designer logos.

The blonde waltzed ahead of the nanny and her children, the little one pushing her new scooter to follow her mother.

"Hurry up, Yolanda," the woman ordered. "And be careful with my purchases. Take them straight to my bedroom."

The entire group disappeared inside the front door of the house.

"W-T-F," Sam said.

"You're not kidding." I was speechless. "Wow."

Five minutes later, Yolanda returned and pulled the car into the garage before closing the door.

"Go get her now!" Sam urged me.

"There's not enough time without causing a lot of commotion," I said. "Relax. She'll be back out."

We sat in my SUV. Sam checked her phone. I did the same.

"Ronnie, we have to rescue Yolanda."

"And what do you suggest we do?" Sam wasn't the patient type when it came to surveillance.

"I have to think about it," she mumbled.

The front door opened and Arianna peeked out. She pushed her pink scooter through the door and got on it. There were no pedals, so the little girl pushed with her feet to get herself over to the long driveway which sloped downward toward the street.

"Oh-oh," Sam said.

"Where's Mom?" I looked frantically back at the door.

We both watched in horror as the child positioned herself on her scooter at the top of the driveway. Her feet were firmly planted on the ground while she looked down the sloping pavement toward the street and then left and right, as if she were deciding her next move.

The nanny popped out the door and called out, "Arianna! Wait!"

The little girl looked over at her, and said proudly, "Look, Yolanda, I can ride by myself." She smiled with glee as she picked up her feet and put them on the scooter's small built-in running boards. The scooter started rolling downhill.

"Wheeeee," Arianna yelled.

Her expression rapidly changed to one of fear as she picked up speed. Yolanda ran to the driveway hoping to catch up to her charge, who was now shrieking at the top of her lungs with terror, not joy. This was the moment her mother appeared at the doorway. Observing the unfolding scene, she dropped her enormous tote bag and let loose a string of expletives.

I was ready to jump out of the car—our cover be damned—to do my best to catch Arianna at the bottom if she made it that far.

Now running down the driveway after the screaming girl, Yolanda yelled, "Arianna, turn. Just turn the handle bars."

The child gave them a hard push to the left and the scooter made a sharp turn as it jumped into the grass, rolling slightly uphill, and finally tipping over. The scooter fell on top of Arianna, who was now in a full-blown meltdown of sobs, crying so hard she could barely breathe.

Yolanda swooped in and gathered the girl in her arms. "It's okay, Arianna. You're safe now. Try to breathe slowly." The girl settled down in Yolanda's arms as her foul-mouthed mother came down the hill in a new outfit and combat boots.

"You are fantastic," Yolanda said to Arianna. "You

listened when I called to you, even though you were scared, and you did it. You saved yourself when you turned onto the grass." She gave the little girl a hug and then patted the grass. "And wasn't it much softer to fall on the grass than on the driveway?" Arianna nodded, staring straight into Yolanda's eyes.

"You are so smart," were Yolanda's final words as the mother grabbed her kid by the hand and pulled her away from the nanny.

As they walked up the hill with her mother scolding her, Arianna turned her head toward Yolanda and smiled.

Yolanda gave her a thumbs up, and Arianna gave her nanny one back before she and her mother walked into the house. Yolanda wearily picked up the scooter, climbed up the hill, and also went inside.

The two of us sat in the SUV, speechless at what we'd just seen. Yolanda returned, this time pushing an empty handcart. She pointed a fob at the garage door to open it and rolled the handcart to the back of the Mercedes. Opening the trunk, she heaved file boxes out one at a time.

Meanwhile, the mother came outside and picked up her bag. She walked over to her car, watched Yolanda struggle with the boxes, and didn't lift a finger to help. Instead, she just stood there, her expression one of creepy satisfaction. I remembered the packing and loading of similar boxes back at the factory. It all lent more credence to what the workers at the motel had told us, that something was coming down this evening. As the woman stood there watching Yolanda close the trunk and push the cart piled high with boxes inside, my eyes drifted to her feet.

"Wonder where the boss lady's going that requires those work boots." The boots had some kind of logo and she wore them over black leggings.

Sam rolled her eyes at me. "Those aren't real work boots, they just look like it. They're either Chanel or knock-offs, and looking at this house and that Mercedes, I'd bet on Chanel."

"Chanel?" I asked. I never thought of that designer in the business of clunky footwear, but then again, I don't stay up-to-date on Chanel.

She scrolled quickly on her phone. "Yeah, take a look." She showed me, and there they were for more than two-thousand dollars.

"That's crazy," I sputtered.

The blonde, who looked even tougher now in her new get-up, got into her sedan and backed out of the garage.

"Here's a knock-off version." This time, Sam handed me the phone.

I looked and laughed as I gave it back to her. "I'm with you. She's wearing the real Chanel ones."

The Mercedes pulled onto Chateaux Road and drove away.

"Now would be the perfect time to rescue Yolanda from that bitch and get her over to the motel," Sam said. I pulled away from the curb and slowly drove down the street. "Where are you going? We can't leave her there."

"She's the only adult in the house now that the mother has left for the evening." I picked up speed. "I can't take Yolanda and leave those kids unsupervised. They're too young, and I just won't do it."

CHAPTER FIFTEEN

Driving far too fast in a residential area, I watched the Mercedes drive even faster, putting more and more distance between us. I felt certain the woman was heading back to the factory, and I'd find her there if I followed later. I hit the brakes hard, causing a loud screech as Sam and I flew forward.

"Heeeeyyyy," she shrieked, as I drove the SUV slowly to the curb. "What are you doing?"

First, I made a U-turn. "I'm going back."

"You're going back? To get her?" Her volume was dropping as she calmed down.

"That's right. If I leave her, kids or no kids, she could become another loose end that I can't get to in time."

We turned left and we were back on Chateaux Road driving past all the monstrous houses. I parked two down from the villa in case someone else arrived, someone I might prefer to avoid.

I jumped out. "Keep the car running, and if you see me racing toward you, be ready to hit the gas once I'm in."

Sam slid over into the driver's seat. "Got it."

I walked up to the front door. It had a heavy, brass lion doorknocker and I used it to bang on the door loud and clear.

No one came, nor did I hear anyone inside, no voices. I knocked again and wondered if Yolanda and the girls were out back.

I started to walk around the house to find them, when the enormous door cracked open.

"Hello? Who is there?" an accented woman's voice asked.

"Hi. Yolanda?" I responded, trying to see inside.

"Yes. May I help you?"

"My name is Ronnie Lake."

"Madame, I mean Mrs. Cara, is not home at the moment. May I take a message, or you can come back later."

"I'm not here to see her." I hoped I was giving off a friendly, non-intimidating vibe. "It's you I've come to talk to."

The door opened a little more, revealing an expression of surprise that shifted to nervousness. Yolanda's eyes darted around to see if anyone was with me. As her hunched, defensive posture became more pronounced, so did a growing fear in those eyes, as if she knew the pain of being grabbed and taken away.

Before she could close the door on me, I quickly said, "It's Manuel."

Now the door swung open. Startled, Yolanda's

posture shot up straight to her full height—she was tall, maybe five-ten or six-foot—and her voice quivered as she asked me, "Did something happen to my cousin?"

"Manuel is fine. This morning he was with José, Tomás, and Rodrigo trying to find their papers in New York. They're back but without their papers, and Manuel's been working today at the car wash and will soon meet up with them again. They've all been worried sick about you since you went missing. I'm here to help." I glanced around, concerned about nosy neighbors. "May I come in?"

There was a momentary pause, and I felt she was deciding whether what I said was on the level and, more importantly, that I was on their side, so to speak.

I guess I passed, because she opened the door wider and signaled to me to enter. "Please."

I stepped inside a monstrous foyer with a grand staircase up the middle. All the walls were painted white, and there were no rugs on the floor or carpets up the stairs, no pictures hanging on any walls. It was such a big, empty, cold space, and I wondered if it was a long-term Airbnb rental.

"Come with me." She walked down a hallway to the left.

We entered a kitchen where Yolanda planted herself next to a window that gave her a view of the street and anyone approaching the house.

"Where are the girls? Will they hear us?" I secretly snapped a picture of her with my button camera and a second one for backup.

Surprised that I knew to ask about the girls, she waited a beat then answered anyway. "No. They are upstairs watching movies."

"Will their mother be home soon?"

"Their mother?" She gave me a strange look.

"Yes, the lady in the Mercedes."

"The boss is not their mother." There was an unexpected toughness in her voice.

"You mean your boss, Mrs. Cara—"

"My boss is also the big boss of everything, that's what I mean." She looked out the window. "Madame Cara runs the car washes and a factory for clothes in Paterson."

"I thought Maxim Popov owns the car washes and factory—"

"He owns them," Yolanda said. "She is the manager."

"Are we talking about the same person?" I asked. "The blonde woman who walked out of here fifteen minutes ago in leggings and Chanel work boots? The mother of the two little girls?"

"Yes, and she is not their mother." Yolanda went to the refrigerator and pulled out two bottles of water. "She is a monster who pretends she's the mother." She handed me one bottle and looked me in the eye. "She took them from the real mother when they were really little. I try to protect them, because she is a nightmare to those girls. They are afraid of her."

"So, it's like you're their big sister?" She nodded. I

opened my bottle of water and took a few gulps while I tried to process this new information. "How long have you been missing from the factory...from your friends and family?"

"Ivan and Boris brought me here two months ago to be the nanny, to manage the house, uh, be the housekeeper. There was no time to tell anyone. One day they called me to the office, and we leave." She drank half her bottle. "I'm sorry, what is your name?" Her voice had a toughness in its tone.

"Ronnie Lake."

"Mrs. Lake—"

"Ronnie, please."

"Ronnie, why are you here? Do you have a message for me from Manuel?"

"Something is going down tonight. I don't know all the details, but the bosses are separating some of the women from their families, maybe selling them. So, Manuel and his friends went to Maxim Popov's apartment to find all your passports to make a run for it—" I saw confusion on her face. "Leave very fast with their families. You know, Beatriz, Ana, Carolina, and you. But they couldn't find the papers." I thought the rest of the story concerning Marissa and the deal that Will was working on could wait until later. "I'm here to bring you to them. I have a car waiting for us down the street."

Yolanda stood up in exasperation. "Impossible."

"What do you mean?"

Yolanda pulled me by my arm. "Come with me. There are no documents at Mr. Popov's apartment."

"Do you know who has them?"

We entered a home office off the kitchen.

"My boss has them. Yesterday morning she asked me to come in here, where she always gives me the chores. I saw her looking at many passports on her desk." Yolanda held her hands ten inches apart, indicating a pile of passports. "On two of them, I saw the names of two women at the factory, so I think it's all our passports."

She showed me a secret safe in a supplies closet, indicating that's where the passports were kept. It was locked.

"This morning, when I was cleaning the kitchen, I heard Mrs. Cara talking on her phone. She says to somebody to get ready to move all the workers tonight and hide them. She says to close two car washes for maintenance, and the managers should be the work crews at the open ones."

"I wonder why she wants to move them tonight?" I looked around Mrs. Cara's desk.

"Because ICE is coming tomorrow," Yolanda said.

There it was on Mrs. Cara's desk, a scheduled ICE inspection notice planned for tomorrow. It was the official form from U.S. Immigration and Customs Enforcement, and it was the confirmation of what José had already told us earlier. I snapped a quick picture of it with my phone and texted it to Will to alert him.

Two things appeared to be going down almost at the same time—the sale of some of the women to an outside buyer later tonight and the ICE inspection tomorrow. You'd think they'd have put off the sale of the women until ICE was out of their hair.

"Well, that explains a lot. We need to hurry, too." I stood up to leave. Yolanda didn't move. "Come on, this is serious. The bosses could come for you, too, and include you in that group they're selling tonight."

"They don't want me. I'm too old."

"What are you talking about?"

"I heard Madame speaking on the phone this morning. She said to choose the youngest and prettiest girls to add to the new ones they're bringing from Virginia. That group gets sent to Philadelphia. She said the clients pay lots of money, so she wants them to like what they get and come back to her for more business." Yolanda took a long drink from her water bottle. "I think the girls will sell purses and scarves and sunglasses on the street. That's what I heard her say on the phone, and who knows what else they must do. So probably they send Ana, because she's beautiful."

"If that's the case, then let's go and get Ana from the factory." I tried to take her arm, but she pulled back. "We can save her."

"I do not want to be deported. The boss always says she will deport me if I don't do a good job. My life is much better *here* than in Mexico." She pointed at the ceiling. "A roof over my head." She opened a huge refrigerator that was well-stocked. "When I'm hungry, all this food to eat. And it's better here for Manuel, too. Even with the boss who is a bitch." She sighed and looked away for a moment. Then with resolution, she said, "It's most important to not leave the girls alone."

"I don't know about the girls, but Manuel wants me to bring you." I knew it was a little white lie, but anything to get her out of here.

"I told you, I'm not leaving the girls." That toughness was back in her voice.

"Bring them with you." I headed for the hallway toward the front door. "Go get them, but please hurry."

The sound of car engines interrupted us, and we looked out the window to see a white van with *Super Lux Car Washes, Paterson, NJ* on the side and the black Mercedes motor up the driveway.

"You have to get out of here," she said.

"Wait, let me give you my phone number." I fished in my pockets but couldn't find a card.

"We go now!" Yolanda tried to push me along, and I grabbed a pen by a phone on my way out of the kitchen.

"Do you have somewhere I can write down my number?"

She rushed me to a door at the back of the house. "Follow me. I'll show you a safe way."

"Let me at least write the number on a piece of paper for you."

"No time."

"How about on your arm?" I reached out.

She pulled her arm back quickly. "No, she will see it."

"How about under your tee-shirt where she won't see it?"

In the back hall, Yolanda stopped and lifted up her tee-shirt to reveal an inch of her lean midriff. "Here." She pointed to one side.

As I wrote the number, we heard the front door open and voices coming inside. Yolanda opened the back door and practically pushed me out, whispering, "Go, go. Get out of here fast. They will kill me if they find you here."

I moved through two backyards on the way to my car. As we drove away, I looked back to see several men pushing handcarts piled with packing boxes into the house.

I'd almost gotten Yolanda out of there, and now I could only hope that she'd be alright.

CHAPTER SIXTEEN

"Is Ana okay?" her mother asked, twisting her hands nervously.

"Yes," I reassured Beatriz.

Once back at the motel, I informed Rodrigo and Beatriz that I'd made contact with their daughter Ana at the factory.

"I gave her your message and told her to be ready this evening, that something is going to happen and she should be ready to run." Marissa translated into Spanish. Rodrigo gently put his arm around his wife and spoke to her softly, translating into Portuguese. Beatriz bit her lip with worry. She buried her head on his shoulder.

Manuel was also at the motel, and I told him that we'd accidentally discovered Yolanda working as the boss' nanny. He wanted every last detail, and I told him my conversation with her, trying hard to leave nothing out. Just in case things went south, I gave him the exact address where he'd find her.

I gave Beatriz money, and she bought more takeout

food for the group. It was now late when she returned, and the group waited hungrily as she arranged the food on the table as a sort of buffet.

Will Benson walked into the room, dressed casually in jeans and a jacket. Everyone stared at him, mostly with concern and fear on their faces, perhaps because of his imposing six-foot-four powerful-looking frame and the brown scruff on his face. I quickly introduced him to the group. Their nerves may have been raw, but his smile did a lot to help disarm them.

"I like your new scruff." I gave him a bottle of water and took one for myself.

"Thanks. I thought I'd try it out, see if I like it."

Full disclosure—there was a time when we'd first met and there was a strong connection between us, even though he's fifteen years younger than I am. We finally concluded platonic friendship was best for us, especially since we'd started working together at times. Even so, sometimes when he looked straight at me with his deep blue eyes, I wondered if he still felt that spark. I changed the subject.

"How's Marissa's agreement coming along?"

"I've got a federal prosecutor over in Newark working on it right now." He looked at Marissa with her sister. "I ought to bring her up to speed." I nodded, and introduced him. Sam joined them, sitting down next to Natalia, who was looking sleepy.

Beatriz and I shared a sandwich. She chatted about her daughter, and in her broken English, she described to me how special Ana was, not just her beauty, but in many other ways. Beatriz was worried that Ana's beauty made her an easy target for the bosses at the factory. I told her I had two daughters in their twenties, and I never stopped worrying about them. We nodded, as mothers who understood each other. It didn't matter that we didn't speak the same language. Then she got busy walking around the room, checking to see if anyone was still hungry for more sandwiches, chips, cookies, and drinks.

Will pulled me aside. "Thanks for the text on the ICE inspection at the factory tomorrow. Get a load of this. I also got a tip from a buddy at Paterson PD that ICE is planning a visit to that strip mall where you told me about the nail salon—"

"They're going there, too?" I interrupted. "The nail salon? Today?"

"Before the day is done. The nail salon isn't their target, though. They're doing an inspection at a restaurant in that mall," he said. "Maybe we should get there before they do and pull out the three women, just in case ICE decides to check out any of the other businesses."

"Shouldn't we tell Marissa and Sam?"

"I've already told them."

As we walked outside, Will added, "My friend, Jerry Baldini, from the Paterson PD will meet us there, and—"

"What?! Aren't you jumping the gun—"

"Keep moving. We don't want to get there *after* ICE." Will waved me toward my car. "I'll explain later." He opened the door to his pick-up truck. "Let's go in separate vehicles. Call me and on the way over you can tell me what you know about the women who were taken there."

~~~~~

"Okay Ronnie, bring me up to speed." Will said, his voice coming through the speakers in my car. We'd been driving for about ten minutes.

"Is that you right behind me, or do you have the address in your GPS?" I asked, looking ahead on the road.

"At the moment I'm behind you, but I've got it in my GPS, too," he answered. I glanced in my rearview mirror and could see his truck behind me.

"Earlier, when I was doing surveillance at the car wash, I watched two guys hand off the three women to an SUV. The women had their hands tied, and they were resisting. They were begging and crying. It was all very emotional and frightening for them. I followed the SUV to this nail salon and watched the boss take delivery around back. I also saw money change hands. I don't know if it was payment for the women or payment to the two men for transporting the women."

"Describe the interior of the nail salon," Will said. "And did you notice where the phones were located?"

A traffic light two blocks ahead turned yellow and

then red. Both of us stopped. This time Will pulled up next to me and nodded through his window. "What can we expect when we go inside?" his voice boomed through my phone speaker. "What's the layout?"

"You walk into a small waiting area with a few chairs and a reception desk on the right. That's where you let them know what kind of manicure you'd like," I said. "There's a cordless landline on that desk, as well as a cell phone. It's where the boss sits—her name is Luciana—but she's on her feet a lot. Anyway, when you walk around this divider, there are pedicure stations on the right and manicure stations on the left."

We continued driving and talking back and forth over our speakers.

"You got that heel tracker in your boot that you love so much turned on?" he asked in a slightly teasing tone.

"Yes, I do have it on, Will Benson, as a safety precaution."

"That's good," he said.

"As a woman PI, when I'm in the field I need to be careful in a way that you don't," I answered. "It's as simple as that."

"Sounds like a useful tool, really," he answered. "Besides the three new women, how many other people were in there working?" Will asked.

"Two women who gave Sam and me our manicures. We tried to make conversation, but they seemed nervous, and Luciana watched everyone like a hawk. I'm not sure they spoke much English. Across from us, there was another woman giving a customer a pedicure. Oh, and there was another employee giving a pedicure to a male customer in a private room where they also served him lunch."

"What about the three new women from the car wash?" Will tapped on his steering wheel. "What were they doing on their first day?"

"One is about forty, and I've since learned her name is Carolina. She's the wife of one of the four men who went to Popov's apartment this morning. When I was in the salon, the boss had her sweeping up around the place and bringing lunch in to the private client. She's wearing a maroon and white dress. She has short black hair with a silver streak in her cowlick. The other two are much younger, almost kids. One has black leggings with sneakers and long, dark brown hair in a messy bun. They had her sitting at a table organizing the bottles of nail polish."

"And the third girl?" he asked.

"Hey, why are you signaling to turn left?" I asked. "I'm going straight."

"It's my GPS telling me to go left. Why aren't you going left?"

"Ignore that," I insisted. "I remember the way. It's not that much further."

"And the third girl?" he repeated.

"She tried to escape before she even got inside the building. One of the guys grabbed her ponytail and slammed her to the ground. Then he slugged her, knocking her out. They put her in a room down a small hall on the right. Poor baby, I hope she's okay. She's got to be scared to death." I shook my head. "The one with the black leggings tried to make a run for it, too, out the back, but the boss lady yelled for this guy and he brought her back. She may be locked up for all I know."

"Anything else we should know about the layout?"

"One more thing," I answered. "There's a back door at the end of one hall, and that hall has a restroom and some other rooms, at least one for private pedicures. There's a second, dead-end hallway off to the right if you come in the front door. It has no exit, but it may be where the two younger girls are stashed, if we don't see them out front in the salon."

Will summed up as we drove into the parking lot of the strip mall. "Two people running the place—the woman at the front desk and the younger guy."

"I think she called him Ralph, no, Rafael," I said. "He had a cell phone, too, in his back jeans pocket."

"Okay, Luciana the boss, Rafael, four employees already there working, and the three new ones from Paterson."

We parked next to each other in the middle of the front lot where we had a good view of the entire mall. As we put down our windows and clicked off our phones, we both looked toward the restaurant. Things looked pretty quiet and dark outside, even with the lighting surrounding the lot.

"It doesn't look like ICE has arrived yet," Will

noted. There was little activity except for a few diners coming and going and two customers picking up take-out as we watched for the next ten minutes.

Our focus shifted as a woman walked into Bella Vida Nail Salon. Another came out, got into her car, and drove away.

Will's phone buzzed and he picked it up. "Hey, Jerry, we're parked out front. You getting close?" A pause as he listened. "No sign of ICE yet. Things are pretty quiet here." More listening. "Okay, so you'll be out back, and we'll coordinate once you're here. See you in ten."

Then a man in an athletic track suit and a puffer vest exited through the front door of the salon. He was very tall, slouching as he walked barefoot in slides. He looked around nervously, hastily moving to his car and dropping his keys along the way.

"Oh, he might be one of the private pedicure clients," I added, looking at the man.

The salon door exploded open and I recognized my manicurist Valentina from this morning as she shot through. She ran after the man, screaming at the top of her lungs. The man had bent over to retrieve his keys, and she slammed into him on purpose. He crashed onto the ground, moaning from the impact.

Luciana came out, but she was yelling at the manicurist, not the man. Valentina answered and they quickly got into an argument that included a lot of arm-waving at each other.

Meanwhile, the dazed-looking man quietly got up and almost crab-walked to stay small and not attract the attention of the two angry women. He successfully made his escape to his car and wasted no time getting away.

The boss slapped Valentina across the face, which shocked her. She froze on the spot. Luciana used that moment to grab her roughly by the arm and drag her back into the salon.

"Whoa, that was certainly extreme, whatever that was about," I commented.

"That boss's behavior certainly fits the possibility that those employees are working there against their will."

All of a sudden, lights in the salon were dimming, and the most recent customer left. "Looks like they're closing early. Maybe that commotion set things off. Come on, Ronnie, let's go."

We got out of our cars quickly. "What's our plan?" I asked.

"You go round up the three women we want, and I'll secure the phones."

We walked fast, which didn't slow Will down from tapping out a message on his phone.

"What about the owner and Rafael? And Jerry?"

"I'm texting him that we can't wait, and we'll improvise with Rafael and the owner." Will tucked his phone in his back pocket, and I did the same. "You ready to defend yourself if you have to?"

CHAPTER SEVENTEEN

I pulled open the door. Will walked through first, and I followed.

Luciana came from around the partition. "I'm sorry, we close early tonight."

"I'm not here for a manicure or a massage," Will answered.

But she ignored him, whipping past him, distracted by me skirting around the partition. "Hey! I know you."

"I don't think so," I responded quickly and kept moving.

But she'd recognized me from earlier in the day, even though Will still tried to get her attention. His voice no-nonsense, he said, "I have other business to discuss with you—"

She waved him off and followed me. "Excuse me—"

I glanced back at Will, and with her attention now on me, he grabbed her cell phone from the desk, as well as the cordless handset to the landline. He tucked her cell in his jeans pocket and the handset in his jacket pocket.

I immediately saw the four women cleaning their pedicure and manicure stations. The older of the three women from the car wash came out of a supply closet near the rear of the salon with a couple of spray bottles and sponges.

"Carolina!" I called. She stopped abruptly and stared at me. "José sent me to bring you back to him."

Her expression was wary, and I could hardly blame her. The women cleaning their stations stopped to watch how this was going to play out.

I swept my fingers through my hair in the spot where her streak was as I said, "José said you have had a grey streak in your hair since you were twenty-five." She felt her grey streak and smiled at me.

"You should come with me." I held my phone out to Carolina so she could contact José. "Call him and I'll get the two others. Where are they?"

The boss surprised me by stepping between us and grabbing my phone. As soon as she did, I grabbed her wrist, using my arm closest to her to get her into position to attack her elbow and straighten her arm. This move caused her to fall down on her knees. She screeched in pain like a bad violin. All it would take was a little more pressure to turn this arm-bar into a hyper-extended elbow, and I could break her joint. She screamed and attempted to regain her balance even as I continued to apply pressure.

I grabbed her hand with my other free hand and twisted it to the point where she had to let go of my phone. She screamed again that I was breaking her arm. Quickly, I used more of my weight to lean in towards her shoulder and this time she fell all the way to the floor as I drove my knee into her back. This Aikido lock on her arm immobilized her, and her earsplitting shrieks continued. Carolina picked up my phone and rushed to the front of the salon, out of our way, so she could call her husband and tell him she was okay.

The boss yelled for Rafael as Will grabbed a set of keys from one of the desk drawers. Rafael shot out from the smaller hallway and Will, who was close by, stuck his foot out. His timing was perfect, and the move sent Rafael crashing to the floor in the middle of the salon. The hard landing momentarily dazed him.

With keys in hand, Will pulled the boss lady up off the floor and pinned one of her arms behind her. This allowed him to maneuver her into the smaller back hallway, where I could hear him banging on doors. "Anyone in there?" he yelled repeatedly.

"Carolina, you stay with me." I held out my hand and she took it. We waited for Will by the front reception desk.

Then I heard young, female voices crying out to Will for help. "Hang on," he yelled back. "I'll get you out."

Rafael moaned as he got up. I watched him, ready in case he made a move for us. He ignored me, and instead spoke to the women at their stations, trying to shoo them toward the back of the salon and gather the group.

They weren't cooperating but looked at each other instead, as if this were a do-or-die moment to get out of there. Then he tried to push them along and got a lot of resistance and arguing.

I could hear the keys jangling in the hall. Using a much gruffer tone, Will demanded, "Which key opens this door?" Silence. "Don't make me repeat myself." Silence.

A woman's groan. Will must have been pushing on the woman's arm that he pinned behind her back. "Stop. Stop," she pleaded.

I heard Will inserting a key in the door.

"What are you doing?" Luciana squawked at Will. Her protests continued but faded, and I guessed he'd pushed her into the room.

Carolina and I wanted to get closer to Will, but I didn't want us to get trapped in that narrow hallway if Rafael had something up his sleeve, so we nervously stayed put.

The door in the small hall slammed loudly and I heard the boss scream at Will at the top of her lungs.

At the same time, Rafael thrashed around the rear of the salon, still attempting to gather and push the other four women toward the hall to the back door. As he did so, his cell phone slipped out of his back pocket and fell onto the floor.

"Stay," I ordered Carolina, and made a dash to the phone. I dove for it, just as he realized his cell was missing.

As I fell to the floor and grabbed Rafael's phone, I felt him jump on me and pound at my midriff with his fists. I did my best to tuck the phone underneath my body, and all that did was make him pound harder as I unsuccessfully struggled to get out from under him. I tried to roll from side to side to get him off of me.

I was aware in my peripheral vision that Will had popped out of the hall with the two younger girls following.

I tried to push my body up, but nothing was working. I felt trapped under Rafael's dead weight, his arms punching me and flailing as he tried to recover his phone. There wasn't much I could do other than keep a tight grip on his phone, but I didn't know how much longer I could hold out.

Next thing I knew, Will pulled Rafael off of me and threw him into the wall. I could see Will really wanted Rafael to come at him so he could finish him off once and for all. I got up off the floor, aching from Rafael's punches, and looked him in the eyes, but he looked away and glanced at Will. He was clearly afraid of Will and made the decision to make a run for it rather than fight to get his phone back.

He turned all his attention to the four women who had been working at the salon. He could see from their faces—and I could, too—that they were ready to bolt.

He harangued them loudly in Spanish, and they retreated in fear as he corralled them down the hall to the back door. Will and I moved carefully toward the front door, protectively shielding our three women in case Rafael changed his mind and made a move on them, too. We didn't want to leave the other four women behind, and I hoped Jerry was close by.

Rafael yelled something to the woman closest to the door, and she pushed it open. He rushed all of them through as a police siren wailed in the distance, getting closer.

The door banged shut.

"That's Jerry, for sure," Will said. "Rafael won't get far because those four will slow him down." He was tapping on his phone again.

I ran to the back, relieved to find an inside lock. I threw the deadbolt, in hopes that would help trap Rafael outside behind the mall.

"What about the phones?" I asked.

Will said he'd put all three in the bottom left drawer and pushed them as far back as they would go. "I texted Jerry where to find them."

We heard someone trying to open the back door. When that didn't work, the first bang made the two younger women jump. He continued banging on the door and kicked at it ferociously. The youngest one with the ponytail began to sob.

"Come on. Let's get out of here." I put my arm around the one who was crying, and we pushed open the front door. This was just as Luciana screamed a new round of verbal threats at us through the walls and banged at that locked door in the smaller hall. Will quickly led the other two outside.

All appeared to be quiet in the entire strip mall, and nothing was going on around the restaurant at the other end. We helped the women climb into my SUV.

As we rolled past the various businesses in the mall, two unmarked cars drove in and parked across from the restaurant. I made a left out of the empty lot to head back to the motel with Will following in his truck. I looked in my side mirror and watched a couple of guys enter the building, and my phone buzzed at the same moment.

I clicked on the speaker and Will's voice came through.

"Perfect timing for us to leave. ICE just pulled in to inspect that restaurant."

"How can you tell? They look like everyday guys picking up take-out."

"I recognized one of them," Will said. "He didn't see me."

"Hey, can we roll around the back and see if Jerry caught up to Rafael with the other women?" I asked. "What if he needs some help?"

"He doesn't need our help, take it from me—"

"I'd just like to know how things worked out for those other four women," I said. "Will they get deported if the police catch up to them?"

"Paterson PD isn't looking to arrest them. They're after the big dogs."

"But Will—"

"Stay focused Ronnie. Let's finish our work here, which is to bring these ladies back to Marissa."

"But Will, what will happen to—"

"Ronnie," he interrupted kindly. "You can't save everyone."

CHAPTER EIGHTEEN

Carolina reached my mobile to me from the back seat where she'd been texting José. "Thank you for letting me use the phone. And for finding us and bringing us to our families."

Ahead of me, Will pulled away in his truck on our way back to the motel. I drove at a slower pace with my three passengers. Along the way, I learned the other women's names—Maria and Suzi—and a little about them.

Fifteen-year-old Maria, the one who got knocked out when she tried to run, was from Venezuela. She'd been separated from her brother at the Mexican border. Left alone and scared, her journey into trafficking began innocently when a kind, older man, who reminded her of a favorite uncle, spotted her and offered to help. His so-called help was anything but.

Seventeen-year-old Suzi had also tried to escape from the salon. I was surprised to learn she was born in this country, specifically in Phoenix, of all places, but orphaned at age twelve when her parents died in a car crash. Social services had separated her from her younger siblings. She landed in one foster family after another and a year ago, she ran away from her last set of foster parents, who were abusive and kept her locked up.

Breaking out, she'd escaped and landed in a shelter by pretending she was nineteen. She'd found work as a babysitter and housekeeper, only to discover she was the family's literal slave. Her six-month tenure ended when they sold her, the final step that launched her into the world of trafficking.

My phone buzzed and I pressed the button on the dash to answer it.

It was Will with news. "I heard back from the U.S. Attorney's office in Newark, specifically the unit that handles organized crime and gangs. They also handle trafficking, and as we speak, we're expecting a draft email for Marissa and me to look over. Maxim Popov's a big catch. He's been on their radar for quite some time in New York, and lately in New Jersey, because his businesses in Paterson are much more recent. They'll be working hand-in-hand with the asset forfeiture unit, too."

"Amazing, Will, thank you."

"Oh, one last piece of good news," he added. "My contact also mobilized several service organizations—a legal aid group, a housing organization, a food bank, a social worker to get these people going with other services."

"That's fantastic. Marissa must be very happy," I said. "Are you already at the motel?"

"I just pulled in," he said. "Are you right behind me?"

"I'll be there in five."

"I'll be in the room looking over the agreement with Marissa."

"Okay. Bye."

We arrived at the motel and I parked close to the room. José carefully looked out the door next to Marissa's room. Carolina jumped out of the car while he simultaneously threw open the motel room door, and they ran to each other. They embraced and kissed, looking happy and relieved to be back together.

Sam had followed José out. "Marissa paid for another room, because we figured a few more people might end up here."

I waited for the two younger women to get out of the car. "Sam, come meet Maria and Suzi." The girls looked nervous and smiled at Sam shyly. They looked at me for guidance on what was happening next. I took one look at Sam in her brightly patterned leggings, long red hair, and crooked smile—how could anyone resist such an engaging, approachable, one-person welcoming committee?

"Girls, you go with Sam until we get everything figured out. She'll take care of you."

"Hi Maria. Hi, Suzi." She waved them in. "We've got food. We've got cable. We've got movies.

Everything's gonna be okay. Follow me." She grinned as they all went inside.

I leaned against my SUV and texted Will that I was outside. I checked my phone for the status of the trackers—my FitBit and the ball cap I'd given to Ana and the tracker I'd put underneath the truck at the factory. All three were at the factory. Nobody was moving yet.

I heard a door open, and I glanced up as Will came over.

"How's the agreement coming along?" I asked.

"It's almost done. Just a few minor changes," Will said. "I think we're good to go."

Even though he already had my text of the ICE inspection form, I shared more details of my conversation with Yolanda at the house. I passed along what she told me about how the factory and car washes were prepping for their inspection the next day.

"You couldn't get her out of there?" he asked.

"You don't know how hard I tried, Will, but she wouldn't leave the two kids she takes care of and Mrs. Cara came home with some other people. It would have been too risky." I took his phone and entered the Chateaux Road address.

"We'll have to pick her up later," he said.

Just then, a car I didn't recognize drove in and parked on the other side of the lot. Before I could say a word, Will spoke up.

"Rossi's going to help out—"

"What!" I exclaimed and stopped walking.

"Detective Rossi? What is she doing here, this isn't where she works."

"Rossi grew up in Paterson. You didn't know?" he asked, faux innocence dripping from his voice and a little smile playing around the corners of his mouth. I could tell he just loved delivering this piece of news to me about the officer who most of the time viewed me as an annoyance when our paths crossed professionally.

"Okay, so she's born and bred Paterson. So what?"

"Rossi still lives here, and she's got a few days off. I called her for help." Will stared at me with those piercing blue eyes. "And she's helping."

"Just my luck," I muttered, looking toward her car, but she didn't get out...maybe busy with her phone. I realized my teeth were clenched, so I relaxed my jaw.

"Be nice." Will had that tone in his voice that I knew only too well.

Another unmarked car pulled in and parked near Rossi. A man got out.

"Who's that?"

Will looked over. "Oh, good—"

"I thought we were going to keep this small," I complained.

The man signaled for four women to get out.

"Jerry just texted me—Rafael and Luciana are in custody," Will said. "His partner's taking care of them, and Jerry brought these four here to join the group once he'd switched to his unmarked car. He's going to assist us."

Will waved Jerry and the manicurists from *Bella*

Vida Nail Salon toward the second of the two doors. It opened, and I could hear Sam's exuberant voice welcoming them, too.

Detective Jerry Baldini came outside a few minutes later, and Will quickly introduced me to his Paterson PD friend. Probably in his mid-forties and dressed in plain clothes, Jerry had a brown mustache just like Tom Selleck in his *Magnum P.I.* TV days. When he smiled, his eyes even crinkled like Tom Selleck's.

Baldini looked over at his car as Sofia got out of hers, still staring at her phone. He called out, "Hey Rossi," and her head jerked up. "How ya doin?" She gave him a nod and then a huge smile. I wondered if she'd ever noticed the resemblance between Baldini and Selleck. Probably not—she was too young for that era.

She strolled in our direction. "Hey, Jerry, Will." There was a very pregnant pause before Rossi acknowledged me. "Hello, Lake." It was an understatement, of course, that Rossi's greeting for me wasn't as enthusiastic as the one for Will and Jerry.

"Hello, Rossi," I said back. I gave her a mega-smile, which I could count on to annoy her most of the time.

Will looked at his phone. "Okay everybody. It's after nine. Let's get over to the car wash and set up before the ten o'clock hand-off."

~~~~~

We got in place at the Super Lux Car Wash and scattered our parking. Will waited with me in my car and Sofia with Jerry in his. We were positioned so that we could see anyone enter or leave. While we waited, I brought Will up-to-speed on the trackers I had in place under the truck at the factory and with Ana. I guided him on installing the apps for the truck and the ball cap so he could keep track on his phone, too.

There were still a few cars pulling in for a wash. I kept my eye out for the same beige van with the dent in the door. Nothing. I watched for the same amethyst-colored SUV. Nothing. In between cars driving in, I fished around in my bag for my binoculars, and my ring bumped up against something hard. I felt it and knew right away it was an extra tracker I'd thrown in my tote before leaving the motel.

Will looked at the small black box. "What have you got that for?" He almost sounded grumpy.

"Hey, a P.I. should never be caught without a tracker if the situation arises." I opened the magnetic case that attached to the underside of a car. It held the cigarette package-sized box that housed the actual GPS.

"Come on, Ronnie. How many of those things do you own? You've already got two on Ana and one on that truck—"

"And weren't those smart moves, Will Benson?" I tucked it back in my tote.

"Okay, okay. What are your plans for that one?"

"I don't know yet. I just remembered I had it."

I texted Juliana that I would not be home tonight in time to pick up Warrior. She sent back a thumbs-up.

It was now ten o'clock, and business had died down to a trickle. Some of the guys left and a couple of others took their place, but from what Yolanda had told me, they were probably bosses from the other car washes. It felt like everything was winding down in order to be ready for the ICE inspection the next day.

By ten-thirty, the crew closed up the place instead of offering their regular twenty-four-hour service. They left and we stayed, continuing our surveillance.

Ten minutes later and a half dozen blocks behind us, a black SUV raced down the street.

"Stay cool," Will said into his radio to Jerry and Sofia. "Let's watch what they do."

It was fast enough that it screeched on the turn into the car wash. The centrifugal force actually tipped the vehicle off two of its wheels. The SUV righted itself and landed hard.

CHAPTER NINETEEN

The driver braked fast and the vehicle stopped over to the side behind the car wash. He parked it next to a thick hedge. All remained quiet for the next fifteen minutes, as if he was waiting for something to happen, too.

Finally, a small, skinny, greasy-looking guy tipped out. He was bent over and groaning and swearing. He slowly straightened himself out, shaking his arms and legs and then stretching his contorted body.

"Is he the only one?" I whispered, more to myself than anyone else.

He leaned against the bumper of his car and lit a cigarette, enjoying his smoke with long inhales and large smoke circles on the exhale. I pulled out my binoculars and focused on the lower front of the car.

"He's got New York plates." I tried to see into the windows with little success. "I'm guessing he's by himself."

Suddenly he broke down into a fit of raspy, deep coughing. It was so fierce, it hurt to listen to him even with the windows up. It went on and on, probably a smoker's cough. He eventually recovered and continued puffing.

After the guy finished his smoke and tossed the cigarette, he went to the back of his vehicle and dug something out. He came around front, squatted down, and switched out the license plates. I looked again through my binoculars.

"Now he's got Pennsylvania plates." Then he did the same in the back, although we couldn't really see.

"He could be waiting for delivery of the women," Jerry said quietly through his radio.

The man came back around front and as he reached for the driver's door, he froze and then his body jerked as if he were heaving. He made a mad dash around the front of the SUV and shot straight into the bushes.

Will tapped lightly on his window. "I don't think we need to hear the sound effects of him throwing up."

"Correct, but I could jump out and put this extra tracker on the bottom of his SUV." I pulled it out of my bag. "That might really help us—"

"Absolutely not," Will snapped at me. "Law enforcement has to get a court order allowing them to use one, and you've already got one on that other truck."

"Well, I'm not a police officer," I said, "so the rules don't exactly apply." Will opened his mouth to respond, but I jumped back in quickly. "I'm not doing it, okay? I'm sorry to upset you, but I can't promise it won't happen again."

He closed his eyes and shook his head. "Ronnie, Ronnie, Ronnie."

I opened the tracking apps on my phone. "You know the truck I told you about with the blankets and bottled water?" I asked. Will nodded. "It's on the move."

He opened the app on his phone, too.

Finally, the old guy came out of the bushes looking kind of shaky. He turned his back on us to climb into his SUV, started up the engine, and drove off.

"It looks like a no-go here at the car wash," Jerry said through the radio.

"Ten-four," Will responded.

"Whoa," I continued, "It looks like Ana's still at the factory according to my FitBit app, even though the ball cap tracker is on that truck. So, which is it? Is she at the factory or on the truck?"

Will clicked on his radio. "Jerry, can you and Rossi meet us down the block?"

Everyone quietly moved out of position, got into their own vehicles, and reconvened further down the street. Will instructed everyone to check the tracking apps.

"As you can see, the truck that was at the factory is moving out," Will said. "They may be transporting the workers to hide them before their ICE inspection tomorrow. You two follow the truck while Ronnie and I check out the factory. We don't want to miss this hand-off of the girls in case there's a change in plans. Keep us posted."

~~~~~

It didn't take long to find ourselves back on the street, driving beneath the overpass that put us almost directly in front of the six-story clock tower building. It was dark except for a light on here and there inside, one of them shining through the window immediately to the left of the big door.

We parked near a coffee shop, got out, and I watched Will slip a gun inside a holster underneath his jacket—his .45 caliber Glock sidearm. He stuck another smaller one in an ankle holster.

I could hardly blame him. We weren't entirely sure if the building was completely empty, except for maybe Ana.

"No weapons?" he asked me.

I pulled a can of pepper spray out of my pocket. "This'll work well if I need it."

"Have you got your handgun license yet—"

"I'm licensed with a shotgun—"

"Well, that's not gonna help around here."

"Oh, one of these days I'll get a handgun…maybe." I crossed the street, and he did, too.

While I pulled on a pair of disposable gloves, Will used a set of tools to open the large side door into the factory. We were worried for Ana's safety, as well as the other girls who were being sent away tonight. As far as we knew, we hadn't set off any alarms. We stayed quiet, and I waved to Will to follow me inside.

The first door on the left was open and light poured into the dark hallway. Since he was the one with the gun, he positioned himself first next to the door and signaled me to get behind him. I kept my pepper spray at my side.

"Ready?" he whispered.

"Ready," I whispered back.

Will burst through the open door, took a shooting stance, and quickly scanned the small room. "Empty," he said to me as I entered. It looked like a regular office where somebody actually worked. There were a couple of metal file cabinets that had seen better days and two mismatched desks with the usual clutter that is expected in a busy office. It was clean and looked ready for an ICE inspection the next day. Will checked the closets and I looked under the desks.

"Follow me," I said. We continued moving down the hall and entered the small showroom. I flipped on the lights to reveal several clothing racks and a few scattered chairs. All the brightly colored samples hung neatly on the racks, ready for the next day's business...and the inspection.

We kept moving as I opened the door into the dingy room that looked over the factory floor. I flipped on all of the light switches, which lit up the now empty space filled with sewing machines.

"What do you think we're going to find down there?" Will asked as we took the steps that opened onto the floor.

I looked at one of the GPS apps on my phone. "I don't know, but my FitBit says Ana's here, somewhere in this building."

I walked directly to her sewing machine. The brightly-colored dress with the matching chiffon carwash skirt sat bunched up by the machine, as if it had been tossed aside. I picked it up and smelled it.

"You're kidding," Will said. "Do you actually smell anything on that dress?"

"Of course not. I wish I had Warrior here. Maybe he could pick up her scent, and that could help us search the building more quickly." I exhaled in frustration.

I shook out the garment. "Wow." I held it up, shocked. "Somebody did a number on this dress. When Ana showed this to me, it looked perfect. Now, it looks like someone's taken a pair of scissors to it."

"Why would they do that?" He walked over to get a closer look. "And does it mean anything regarding her wellbeing?"

"I hope not." I looked around her station for any other clues. Finally, I gave up.

"Hey, I'm going to see if I can find the dorm where they housed these women."

"Do you even know where to start?" Will asked from across the room.

"Beatriz told me they live on the sixth floor here. I'll see if I can find an elevator, or I'll hoof it up there." I turned toward the stairway. "Can you check each floor and work your way up? If I need you, I'll text or call, and you do the same."

"Getting bossy there, Ms. Lake." He grinned.

I smiled, rolled my eyes, and trotted up the steps.

Once back in the hallway, I found a freight elevator at the other end. I let Will know, closed the heavy top and bottom doors, and hit the button to climb to six. I rode up in the dark—except for my phone flashlight—as the old lift bumped and groaned, slowly making its way from floor to floor. It felt like forever, and about the time I was wishing I'd taken the stairs, it shrieked and clunked a few times against the wall surrounding the cage as it banged to a stop.

It took a moment to open the gate, and I stepped out. It was pitch black, so I shined my flashlight around until I found switches to one side of the elevator. I pushed them up and a half dozen dim bulbs hanging from the ceiling flipped on one by one.

I gazed up at what I estimated to be twenty-foot-high ceilings. Thick wooden beams filled the space above my head. I scanned the entire floor and noted all the framing running down both sides of the space. Some of the framing had old sheet rock sloppily nailed to it, creating unfinished rooms.

I walked down the middle of the space on rough old floorboards, counting maybe thirty cots, quite a few out in the open and others tucked in corners where the torn, dirty sheet rock created areas of privacy. Here and there were a couple of cots near each other. Perhaps they were for mothers and daughters—I remembered the woman at her sewing machine worriedly watching the younger girl being led off the factory floor by one of the bosses.

Why were all these cots empty? There were no mattresses, sheets, or blankets. There were a few chairs scattered nearby. They were empty of the clothing that should have been draped on them, and there were no shoes tucked under the beds. Little tables near the cots were empty of hair brushes, toothbrushes in glasses with toothpaste alongside, or dishes with bars of soap. Maybe the toiletries were in a bathroom.

I looked around and saw small built-out areas in two of the four corners of the loft. I went over to one, flipped on the light switch, and opened the door to a room with light grey walls—not from the paint color but from accumulated dirt over many years. Simultaneously, the terrible stench of a stopped-up toilet slammed into me, almost making me step back through the door. I walked across ancient linoleum that was supposed to look like tan-colored tiles and over to the tan-colored toilet where I flicked the lid down.

I tried the faucets of the sink and cloudy, stinky water splashed into the basin, slowly going down a clogged drain. It smelled like rotten eggs or sewage, and I turned my attention to a shower stall with a cracked smoked glass door. That faucet splattered water on a tile floor that was so dirty it was scary even imagining stepping on those tiles barefoot.

Overall, the place was filthy, and there were no personal toiletries anywhere to be seen. I walked over to the other built-out area to find a duplicate bathroom, just as dirty and empty as the first one. I looked out over the dormitory—only these two small bathrooms for more than twenty women who worked very long hours and probably perspired heavily in that overheated shop.

Goosebumps made me rub my arms. It may have been hot on the factory floor, but six stories above, it was chilly. How did the workers stay warm at night? I'd noticed noise from a few ancient radiators built against the walls, probably from when this factory was first constructed in the nineteenth century. I walked over and could feel a little bit of heat coming out of several of them.

Ana's mother had said that she, her daughter, and all the other women in the factory lived on the sixth floor of this building. If this was their dorm, why was there no sign of any of them in this space, no personal belongings? My working theory? The bosses had them pack up their things and take it all with them before they got on the truck to leave. If the ICE inspection were to drift up to this floor, the bosses certainly didn't want any sign of anyone living up here. Rather, the impression would be that all their workers went home every night to apartments and houses.

I checked my FitBit app, and it still showed Ana was in the building. It was possible that she'd thrown it out. I wondered if Will had found anything that could lead us to where she was.

I heard the clunking sound of boots and looked toward the stairway next to the elevator. Will's head appeared first and then the rest of him as he trotted up the last few steps.

"Did you find anything up here—" He stopped himself and took a long look from one side to the other. "So, this is where they sleep."

I explained my theory about why there were no belongings, and he agreed that made sense. "How'd you do on the four other stories on your way up?" I asked. "Anything interesting?"

"The second floor is used for storage. A lot of bolts of fabric, machine parts, that sort of thing. The other floors are empty, almost abandoned." He looked around again. "It is strange how cleaned out this space is, since this is supposed to be their dorm."

I looked around again, too. "Well, they probably didn't have much to start with. Maybe not even enough to put in a backpack."

Will walked toward a small door on the other side of the elevator. "What's over here?"

"I don't know. I haven't checked that out yet."

He opened it, turned on the flashlight, and stepped inside. "I don't see a light switch in here."

I walked toward the sweeping beams of Will's flashlight. "What's in there?"

"It's the inside of the clock tower. It's only a couple of stories high."

I stepped through the door into a claustrophobic twelve-by-twelve space with a wooden ladder-combo-staircase zigzagging up to the clock. Will was up top checking it out and then swept his light around one more time.

"Nobody here." He quickly descended and turned off his light as we walked back into the large dorm.

My eyes swept across the loft one last time, and I saw a small flash in one darker corner. I mentally marked the spot, turned my phone flashlight back on, and made my way in that direction.

Will followed. "What did you see?"

"I saw a quick flash over in that corner. I want to check it out. Come on."

We walked across the creaking wooden floor. I slowed down as we got to the corner. I stood still for a moment, waiting, and hoping for another flash to guide me. There were two cots placed in a loose "L" formation. Probably two family members or two friends slept here.

I swept my light around the area and then under the first cot. Nothing. I swept the light under the second one and almost missed something showing partially behind one of the legs of the cot. It looked like a scrap of fabric. I scooted around and reached for it, and that's when I got another small flash through the fabric. It felt like a bangle, and at the same moment I knew.

"Will, this is my FitBit!" I unwrapped it from the fabric and shined my light on it. "What's it doing here?" I checked the back of the band for a scratch that should be there. It was. I couldn't hide my disappointment or the quiver in my voice. "It's supposed to be with Ana."

I swept my flashlight over and under the two cots and around the wider floor area surrounding the beds in case I'd missed something else.

"Are you sure it's yours? I mean, it's doubtful, but maybe one of the other women had one." He reached for it and I handed it to him.

I fingered the cloth that had been wrapped around it as I walked back into the better light of the room. It was the see-through colorful chiffon material Ana had used to make the dress she'd shown me just hours go.

"The FitBit is definitely mine."

Will checked his phone. "The truck is at a warehouse on the outskirts of Paterson. Jerry texted me. He's brought in backup, and it's going down soon."

"What about Ana—"

"You said the ball cap tracker was moving with the truck. She could be there. Come on, let's go!"

CHAPTER TWENTY

Twenty minutes later and two blocks away, Will and I could already see the flashing lights of several police cruisers on one side of an old warehouse in an industrial neighborhood. Two officers dragged a man out of the driver's seat of a truck, patted him down, and handcuffed him. There were a number of other men in handcuffs surrounded by officers. One of two side-by-side enormous garage doors was open, and the truck sat close by parked alongside the building. As we pulled up, I could see people milling about in the shadows inside.

Will and I nodded at Detectives Jerry Baldini and Sofia Rossi, who stood near the open warehouse door with a woman and a man who held a clipboard and pen.

Jerry introduced me—Will already knew them—to Martina Diaz and Tom Spenser from a local nonprofit organization. Baldini had worked with them in the past and Will had suggested them to Marissa. They were there to help the car wash and factory workers get set up with services to start their new lives. I'd assumed everyone in the group was undocumented and was surprised to learn that several were U.S. citizens, but like Suzi with the sloppy bun at the nail salon, had been swept up into trafficking at a young age.

Martina and Tom quickly mingled with the workers. She took group pictures of several at a time with her phone, mostly speaking in Spanish as Tom wrote down pertinent information. They had several other team members doing more of the same.

"They're mostly doing a head count before they transport them to a safe location," Baldini said.

"Remember, there's another group already at the motel that should be included in the final count," I said, looking around for Ana.

Will looked up from his phone. "Good news, Ronnie. Marissa has a final email agreement with the feds. They're going after her father, and she's doing a really great service by stopping this group of traffickers and helping these people."

I went inside as Will and Sofia walked over to one of several Paterson Police Department cruisers to speak with an officer. I scanned the forty or fifty people and couldn't spot Ana. I looked for the two teenaged sisters from Honduras to ask them if they'd seen Ana. I couldn't find them either, so I walked slowly through the crowd, asking the women if they'd seen Ana or the two sisters.

In one cluster, a woman who spoke little English switched to Spanish when talking to her friend. The only words I understood were Ana Braga's name. I pulled Martina over for help.

The woman repeated what she'd said to me, and Martina translated. The woman pointed to the back of the building and waved at all of us to follow toward a smaller garage door.

"Alma says when they came here on the truck maybe twenty minutes ago this door was open," Martina said. "Ana and the two sisters, Inès and Luna, were with this larger group."

"From Honduras? With long hair?" I asked Alma, using my hands to indicate the sisters' hair.

Alma nodded in agreement. "Yes, yes." She continued in Spanish.

"There was a lot of confusion when they got here," Martina translated. "One minute they were here, and Alma turned away for some reason. And when she turned back a few moments later, she saw them being pushed into a black SUV by an old guy and another man, a big guy waving a gun."

"Where?" I asked in a panic.

Alma pointed to the garage door at the back of the building speaking in Spanish. Martina said, "Right outside that door."

I pulled my phone out and checked the app for the ball cap with the GPS. It was moving away from our location. "There she goes," I muttered. "I can get her."

I ran outside, got in my car, and was almost ready to pull out when Will and Rossi reached me. "Slow down," he said. "Where do you think you're going?"

"Ana and the two sisters were taken away from here," I said in a hurried tone. "And if I leave now, I can get to them."

"You don't know that," Rossi said.

"I can definitely do this." I snapped back at her. "The people who bought her are putting her on the street to sell stuff. I have this from a reliable source."

Will disagreed. "You don't know what you're getting yourself into. There's been no surveillance yet, nothing. You could be walking into the middle of a dangerous situation. You don't even know if they have guns."

"There are two men in the SUV that took the girls," I answered. "I think one was that old guy we saw at the car wash. He must have picked up the other one, a bigger guy with a gun on the way over here—"

"That settles it," Will said. "Rossi, you go with Ronnie—"

"I don't need a babysitter," I asserted.

"I didn't say that. Look, Rossi's coming with you," he insisted. "You could run into some unexpected situation and be glad there are two of you." He looked at Rossi. "You take your car, too."

"Ronnie, do you still have my number in your contacts?" Rossi asked.

"Yes." I found Rossi's cell number and sent her the information on the GPS locator in the heel of my boot. Next, I copied three different photos and sent them in a group text to Will and Rossi.

"What are you doing now, Lake?" Will asked. "I thought you were in a hurry to get out of here."

"I'm texting you both photos of Ana and the two sisters." I looked at Will. "Just in case they turn up around here somewhere. Like, say, they were able to escape close by from that SUV that just hauled them off." Then I looked at Rossi. "And also, so you'll recognize them when we find them."

"Good idea, Lake," Rossi said.

As Rossi walked to her car, I remembered something and said to Will as I scanned the group of undocumented people one last time, "We have another member of this group still off-site."

"Who's that and where do we find him?"

"Her not him. Yolanda. Hernandez. Do you remember Manuel Hernandez, at the hotel?"

Will shrugged, not sure which one he was among the myriad of faces.

"He's one of the guys from this morning at the tower in the city. He and his cousin Yolanda came up from Mexico together. She's been working as a nanny for the boss lady, Mrs. Cara, who runs the car washes and the factory for Popov, and the woman's apparently a nightmare. I tried to pick Yolanda up before we went back to the nail salon."

"What happened?"

"She wouldn't come. She didn't want to leave the two kids alone." I searched for her picture and texted it to Will along with the address on Chateaux Road. "You can arrest her boss at the same time. I don't see either of them here."

"I know, I'll head over right now and pick up Yolanda, and I'll take an officer to arrest the boss, Mrs. Cara," Will said.

"Also, Mrs. Cara has all the workers' passports locked up in an office by the kitchen. They're in a safe in the supplies closet. Yolanda can show you."

"Got it. And you keep me posted on Ana and the two sisters. Don't forget these are dangerous people who've taken her. Be careful."

"I will," I said, knowing that was a hefty promise to keep.

He swatted the hood of my car to get going. "Now get out of here."

CHAPTER TWENTY-ONE

"Sales crew, my ass," Detective Sofia Rossi said as we drove. "Did you say they chose only young and pretty girls? Sounds like a cover for sex trafficking to me."

I could see her behind my SUV in her own vehicle. Once we were on I-80 heading west, I'd shared every detail of what I knew about tonight's sale of the girls. Rossi was definitely not buying it.

We turned south and stuck to the main highways that our app showed us. We finally ended up on I-95 heading west again, but driving faster and this time toward Philadelphia.

Fear motivated us. Fear that Ana's new bosses would toss her into a prostitution pipeline. Fear that they would ply her with drugs. We had to get there in time, hoping that we'd find Inès and Luna still with her.

Our app told us to turn off the highway in advance of reaching the city proper. The tracker led us through narrow streets before we reached an industrial area. We drove to the edge of a huge lot with one lone truck parked behind a big-box store. The black SUV had pulled in parallel but some distance from the truck. I don't know, maybe the truck had nothing to do with why the SUV was there. Rossi and I stayed in the shadows where our cars wouldn't be noticed.

Nothing happened for the next twenty minutes or so.

Finally, a large van drove in and parked along the building near the SUV in a sort of V formation. It was the kind of vehicle you see at an airport, shuttling passengers to car rental lots. The two guys in the SUV pushed out the Honduran sisters, who hung onto their packs for dear life. The skinny, old man reached inside the SUV and then threw something at Inès, the elder of the siblings.

I put down my window and Rossi did the same. Inès was protesting that the hat did not belong to her.

"What?" the old guy whined. "It was on the floor—"

"Ana." Inès called out and tried to get back inside to reach to her friend, but the other big guy stood in her way.

The old man grabbed the cap from her and stuck it on top of her head.

Wait a minute. I looked through my binoculars. Inès now had on the blue ball cap I'd given to Ana. Horrified, I wondered if I'd lost Rodrigo and Beatriz's daughter in all the commotion as the workers were being moved around. We could hear Inès and Luna calling out for Ana.

The girls sounded scared, which was hardly a surprise since they had no idea what lay ahead for them.

Of course, they would try to stay together, and that included keeping Ana with them. I looked through my binoculars again and could see the sisters were crying.

The door to the shuttle made a *whooshing* sound as it opened, and two men with ponytails wearing black leather pants and jackets stepped out. In the windows, new faces looked out to stare at the newcomers. I hurriedly scanned them. They were all young teen girls and some boys, too. The two men pushed Inès and Luna into the van, who by this time were sobbing not to be separated from Ana.

The men climbed up after the sisters and the door closed noisily behind them. A moment later, it made its way across the parking lot.

"It's quick decision time," I said to Rossi. "That ball cap will track the sisters. We no longer have a tracker on Ana, and if we both leave now, we risk losing her for good. You want to follow them and see what's up? I'll wait here until I find out what's going on with Ana."

She paused for a moment, considering this strategy.

"What are you waiting for?" I tried not to let impatience creep into my voice.

She tilted her head slightly from side to side. "Is it time to call in the cavalry?"

"If you do, we risk losing either the sisters or Ana. If we move on one, they could tip off the other one."

"Good point." She stared at me hard.

"Yes?" I asked, and then finally getting it. "I won't do anything stupid."

She still stared at me hard.

"I promise." I stared back at her. "I'll connect with you first. Now get out of here."

"Lake, don't forget that *you're* the rookie." She put her car into drive.

"Yeah, well, you won't let me forget it, I'm sure."

"You got it." She drove away.

~~~~~

It felt like forever. I sat in the car, watching and waiting for something to happen with the parked SUV. Was Ana in that car or not? I started to worry, imagining all sorts of nightmare scenarios. Had she somehow slipped out of the SUV, either forced to or trying to escape, and I'd missed it? I'd never forgive myself if I had. I didn't want to disappoint her parents with the news that they'd never see her again.

I tried to work out a plan where I'd creep up on the SUV to see if I could spot Ana inside. I knew it was a bad idea since it was two against one. Also, one of the men had a gun, and I did not.

It was well after 3 am when Detective Rossi returned. Before we could both completely lower our windows, I picked up the pleasing aroma of coffee. She reached over a fresh cup.

"Thank you, Sofia."

"The sisters are okay for the night."

"How?" I asked.

"I followed the van to an apartment complex and

watched them unload the kids. The boys went into one unit and the girls into another, kind of like dorms at school."

"Did those men go into the apartments, too?" The thought of it made me physically sick.

"Not the girls' dorm, but they are guarding the boys," Rossi answered. "I saw two women in charge of the girls. Really big, strong, and mean-looking. I wouldn't want to cross either of them if I was in that dorm. They could beat the shit out of me, and I'm pretty tough."

"Rossi, for you to say that, this must be really bad. You think they've settled in for the night?"

"Yeah, but right before the lights went out, I got up close and could look in through cracks in the curtains," she said. "The girls got a little supper, but they looked scared. I heard the women bosses talking to each other, that the girls would go out tomorrow morning in teams of two or three selling jewelry and scarves around the bus station in Philly. Probably counterfeit luxury name brands."

"Then they went to bed?" I took a sip of my coffee.

"Yep, and don't forget, we've got the ball cap that Inès is wearing. We'll know where they go."

"Let's hope she keeps it with her, and that her sister stays with her, too." I worried she might stuff it in her pack and forget about it. I sipped my hot coffee and placed the cup in the holder.

"Does she know it has a tracker?" Rossi asked.

"I don't think so. There's no reason Ana would have told her." I gripped the steering wheel and then rolled my shoulders, tight with tension. "I just wish something would happen with that SUV over there so we could be sure we know where Ana is."

The old guy got out from the driver's side, leaned against the vehicle, and smoked another cigarette as if he had all the time in the world.

CHAPTER TWENTY-TWO

An old station wagon careened around a corner, raced across the huge parking lot, and hit the brakes hard at the very last moment; I was sure he'd crash into the black SUV. A balding man in his mid-forties jumped out of the front passenger side, leaving the car running. I grabbed my binoculars.

He shooed two teens out of the back seat and pointed toward a dumpster. The boy went first, rushing behind the large container, and he finished quickly. The girl was next, at first hanging back as she talked to the boy. Just when I thought she wouldn't step behind the dumpster, she did. The girl needed more time than the boy for the bathroom break, of course.

Meanwhile, the large man got out of the SUV and opened a back door. He nodded to get moving, and Ana stepped out, clinging to her pack.

I exhaled with relief. "She's okay, thank goodness."

He hustled Ana over to the balding man by the station wagon and handed her over. That guy hurried her into the back seat along with the two other kids by the dumpster. He slammed the door shut, hopped in behind the wheel, and drove out the same direction from which he arrived. A moment later, the SUV did the same.

"Let's go," Rossi said. She didn't waste a second driving after the station wagon, and I followed her. We rapidly had him in our sights.

He led us right back onto I-95 heading toward Philly. The twinkling nighttime skyline of the city got closer and closer. I had to remind myself that Ana no longer had a tracker, so I'd better focus on her in that station wagon that swerved from lane to lane, even though traffic was still light at this early morning hour. We didn't dare lose sight of her.

Rossi rang on my cell. "If he's making you nervous, I can put on my police lights and pull him over for erratic driving. It's your call."

"I don't want to risk doing anything that might trigger the other group from bolting," I answered. "I don't want to lose those sisters."

"Okay. Besides, if we keep following, there may be more kids we can save."

"I agree."

"We're entering Center City," she said as we took the exit and drove into town.

"I know." I always marveled at the mix of tall buildings whenever I drove into this part of town.

Stay focused, Ronnie, I told myself, appreciative of Rossi for keeping us on the station wagon's tail without them noticing us. We seemed to drive for quite a while—left, right, stop at a light, go straight, and do it all over again, or in some other combination of turns.

Eventually the surroundings changed and street lights illuminated a more downscale neighborhood. A sign said Frankford Avenue as we drove past an intersection with pizza takeout, an insurance storefront, a nail spa, and small grocery before reaching an endless string of row houses, two stories or three. There were buildings that had doors opening right onto the sidewalk and others that had several steps up to a porch, really a stoop with an overhanging roof. It was a jumble of brick and a lot of wood in need of a fresh coat of paint.

My phone buzzed and I clicked on.

"Drive slowly even though there's no one around," Rossi cautioned. "Do not make any fast moves here. There's always someone watching."

I couldn't believe she was telling me this just as we drove by a guy in a knit cap, sweatshirt, and a vest using his tools to pop the lock on a car parked along the curb. At four in the morning, should I have assumed he'd lost his keys or was he stealing the car? That particular Audi model did look like a big step up from the rest of the vehicles on the street.

Two blocks ahead, the station wagon turned onto a smaller street.

"Aren't you surprised that guy hasn't made us yet?" I asked Rossi over my speaker.

Her left blinker flashed. "I'm driving around the

block, just in case. You stay on his tail, but not too close. I'll come up behind you in a sec."

"Stay on your phone." I was embarrassed by the small quiver in my voice.

"Aw, you gonna miss me if I hang up?" She made the left.

I hated admitting to myself, but I felt better knowing I wasn't alone in the middle of the night in this neighborhood following a station wagon with some sketchy guy who had taken Ana against her will. The station wagon turned left again and then two blocks ahead of me pulled into a driveway. "He's stopping," I said to Rossi over the speaker phone.

"Keep driving straight and do NOT slow down so much that he notices you," she advised.

The street lighting wasn't great on these several blocks, and it was hard to see much detail. The driver pulled in between a brown clapboard house and a dirty white multi-unit building. I quickly described the brown house with a ground floor open porch right next to the sidewalk. I told her the dirty white building was set back further from the street.

I rolled past the driveway and caught a glimpse of the guy slamming his door and opening the back before I was once again staring at a mish-mash of row houses. In my rearview mirror, I could see headlights turn onto this street. "Is that you, Rossi?"

"Yeah. Pull over further down the street, and I'll park right behind you."

Rossi checked her gun, a Sig Sauer P365. I knew it was one of the lightest, most compact 9-mm pistols available because I'd been researching purchasing one for myself. I had shotguns at home but still didn't own a handgun, and this one was on my top five list. Meanwhile, I stuffed several zip ties into my pocket and had a last-second thought, remembering youngest daughter Jess's gift when I first got my PI license. I hurriedly grabbed my brass tire deflator from the glove compartment in my car.

Rossi clipped her badge to her belt, pulled out her handcuffs and phone, and texted someone. She waited a moment for a response and sent another text. "I've got a colleague in the department down here, and I've alerted him that we're at the scene of a possible trafficking situation involving minors. I don't have jurisdiction here, so we'll wait for back-up unless there's an immediate concern for safety."

I nodded, and we made our way quietly down the alley in the back. Flashlights in hand, we approached from the rear of these buildings by foot because there was even less lighting here than along the street.

Staying in the shadows, we arrived at the driveway with the station wagon. Rossi went ahead with her gun drawn. I stopped.

"What?" she whispered.

"You go ahead," I whispered back. "I'll catch up."

Instead of following Rossi, who was already quietly circling the brown clapboard house, I veered over to the station wagon. My tire deflator had four pieces screwed together, one for each wheel. I crouched down and screwed one of the valves on each tire, releasing the air in all of them. It wouldn't take long for the wagon to have four flats.

Rossi came around the other side, saw what I was doing, and chuckled. I looked up. "This will now be useless as a getaway vehicle." I nodded at the house. "Anything?"

"They're not in there," she said. "Which leaves this other building. And I think this one has more possibilities. Whatever happens, do not rush in."

"Yeah, yeah, yeah," I muttered.

On the back side of the building, stairs led to three levels of balconies, each running along the entire rear of the building. Those walkways provided access to the entrances of all the apartments. Lights were on in two of the units, one on the ground floor and the other on the top.

"Let's see what's going on here first, if we've finally got the right place." Rossi darted over to the first-floor apartment and glued herself next to the wall by the front door. I followed and she signaled for total quiet. We heard nothing, no talking in the apartment, nobody moving around. Maybe they'd gone to sleep and simply forgotten to turn the lights out in the living room.

Rossi signaled me to follow. We carefully climbed the two flights of steps and moved down the passageway to the other apartment with lights on. There were blinds down but not closed over the large window next to the door. Staying to the side, we could make out that people were moving around inside but not see anyone specifically, just as we could hear them talking low and not make out what they were saying.

I leaned closer from the side and pulled back quickly. "I saw Ana," I whispered.

"Remember, do not rush in." She took her phone out, paused to read, and texted someone. "We've got back-up coming."

That was all fine until we heard the sounds of commotion behind the door, and then a blood-curdling scream.

Rossi booted the flimsy door, splintering it with one firm kick. *So much for not rushing in,* I thought.

The balding man who drove the station wagon was now straddling Ana on the floor with his full weight, a syringe poised over her outstretched arm. They both looked at Rossi and me in surprise.

"Police. Drop it!" Rossi yelled as she entered the apartment with her weapon pointed straight at him.

I stayed by the door as she veered to the side closer to them. The man was frozen, staring at Rossi as she slowly walked toward him and continued shouting orders to drop it.

He didn't drop it. "Make me," he yelled at Rossi as he waved around the syringe. Ana squirmed, trying to stay out of the way of the needle.

As he continued toward her arm with the syringe, I grabbed a lamp from a side table and raised it over my head, the cord unplugging as I pulled. I threw myself toward him, bringing the lamp crashing down on the top of his head as hard as I could. Momentarily dazed, he dropped the syringe and tipped off of Ana to one side.

I kicked the hypodermic under the sofa and reached for Ana to protect her. But the man had recovered enough to pull me away from her. In the background, I heard footsteps and a voice from further back in the apartment call out, "Eddie, what are you doing with that bitch?"

"Lake, you got this?" Rossi demanded as she headed in the direction of the other male voice in a different room.

Eddie swung me around. "I got this," I answered a little too soon.

He back-handed me across my face. Pain shot through my neck as I stumbled backwards. I managed to quickly tuck my leg and roll backwards rather than slamming full-force onto the floor.

As I regained my balance, I tried to stomp on Eddie's arm as he lunged to grab Ana, who was crouching down and hiding next to the sofa. All I accomplished was to make him angrier, and he turned his attention towards me instead of her. He came around to shove me out of the way. I was able to sidestep fast, but he still kept coming. I could tell from the way he swore under his breath that this was the first time a hundred-and-twenty-five-pound woman had given him so much trouble. Then my luck ran out.

"You bitch," and he slugged me in my abdomen. I folded over and grunted noisily from the exhale and pain. I'd totally lost control of the situation and might have just made things worse and put all of us in even greater danger.

A bearded man came from the back of the apartment. "Do I have to handle every—hey, you asshole, she's getting away," he screamed at Eddie.

Where was Rossi? Had something bad happened to her? I could hear police sirens in the distance as Ana ran out of the apartment.

The bearded guy yelled, "Go get her!"

Eddie looked around, bewildered. "Who, Cal, me?"

Cal shook his head at his hopeless associate. "Yeah, you, dipshit. Go get her!"

"What do I do with her?"

"Take her to Roxie's," Cal answered. "I'll take care of this one."

Eddie stumbled out of the apartment, and I headed toward the door, too. I could hear Cal's heavy footsteps coming after me until I heard Rossi's voice.

"Stop," she yelled. "I've got a gun on you." Cal froze. "Put your hands on the table." She checked him for a weapon and pulled out her handcuffs.

"Ronnie, go get Ana!" Rossi called out as she cuffed the man. "I'm waiting here for backup, there are more kids in the back."

I nodded and left. From the third floor, I looked down to see the driver holding onto Ana and circling the station wagon as if he wanted to use it to make a run. I quietly moved along the walkway and down the steps as I watched him assess the flat tires. He heard me and looked up. The sirens were heading our way, and the sound seemed to shock him.

"The police are on their way. Let her go," I shouted. Instead, he pulled a gun and held Ana more firmly as they ran off.

I went after them, fearing for Ana's life and also my own now that I'd seen his gun. On the next block, he began a zigzag pattern to parallel streets or gravel-covered roads wherever there was a break or driveway between the row houses.

I got closer and yelled out again for him to stop and release her. He glanced back at me and tripped while he was running, pulling Ana down with him. He lifted his gun and pointed it at me. I couldn't believe it. He was going to shoot me. I threw myself to the ground as I heard a shot ring out and ricochet off a metal container. I stayed low to make sure he didn't fire at me again.

Eddie dragged Ana to her feet, and I could hear her crying. I also heard footsteps behind me, and Rossi crouched down. "The police are at the apartment. You okay? Have you been hit?"

"No, but that gravel landing sure stung."

I looked up to see Eddie run around another corner, pulling Ana. "Come on," he yelled at her.

"Let's split up," Rossi said. "I'll go left and you go to right, but be careful. Don't let him surprise you."

I ran after Eddie, hoping Ana was doing a good job of slowing him down as he continued his zigzag pattern toward Roxie's, whoever that was.

I caught a glimpse of Rossi on the street as I passed another break in the row houses. I scooted by a large tree and my view of the alley opened up. Eddie wasn't far ahead and he wasn't going much further either. There were several monstrous pieces of construction equipment in his way, including a bulldozer and the largest dump truck I'd ever seen. They were parked next to each other and blocking the narrow alley.

Eddie stared up at the vehicles, probably wondering if he and Ana could climb over them to get out of there. There was little chance of that happening as long as he had the teenager with him. He looked around frantically for his next move, while Ana continued crying.

"Shut up," he ordered. She froze for a moment and then continued with more tears and sobs.

To my left, Rossi climbed over the top of the dump truck and toward the back end, which was closest to Eddie and Ana.

Eddie could barely hold onto his gun because he had his hands full with Ana. I jumped out to distract him from noticing Rossi, shouting, "Release Ana. We've got you covered."

He froze, but then aimed his gun at me. Rossi jumped from about eight feet above him off the back of the truck and landed squarely on top of him. The gun went flying. Rossi tried to break her fall, but she landed hard on her left arm and cocked wrist.

"Shit," she screamed in agony.

Still, Rossi had succeeded in knocking him off his feet, and Eddie took Ana down with him. She used her fists and pounded at him, until he let go. Ana quickly rolled away out of his reach.

I ran over and kicked the gun away. I started toward Rossi, who was off to the side, cradling her left arm. "My wrist," she moaned. Her face was contorted in pain.

Eddie didn't take long to recover, and the next thing I knew, he was coming after me in a rage. He came toward me with such speed and force that the only thing left for me to do was default to the "suicide" throw. Just as he lunged to grab me, I fell backwards in an aikido-type fall. I veered my torso to the side. I avoided having Eddie fall on top of me or hitting my head on the ground.

Eddie was absolutely taken by surprise. Instead of him meeting my resistance, I opened the way for him to fly forward and land facedown. It's like when someone is trying to push all their body weight through a closed door but the door is flung open at the very last moment. His body hit the gravel hard, his head following with a thud. As I jumped up, I could see he was momentarily stunned.

I quickly ran over to Eddie while he was still lying

on his stomach moaning and not clear-headed. Digging my knee into his back, I twisted one of his arms behind him, pushing his elbow up his spine. As he flailed his other arm to get at me, I grabbed that as well and pulled one of my zip ties from my pocket. I managed to cuff his two wrists behind him like Will had taught me.

I looked around and saw Ana standing in the shadows. She ran over to help Rossi as I dragged Eddie toward the construction equipment and pulled another zip tie from my pocket. I attached him to a pipe on the front of the massive bulldozer.

"Sofia, are you okay?" I asked Rossi.

"I don't know, I may have broken my wrist when I hit the ground."

"Do you want me to call 911?"

"No, you take Ana and go. Fast, before the police get here. I've got to stay and secure the scene and the weapon. Plus, I'll have some explaining as to why you and Ana left before they arrived." She cradled her arm. "Move it. Get her back to Paterson and her family. I'll ask the local PD to break up the other group with the sisters and I'll work on bringing them back to Paterson, too."

"How are you going to drive for three hours with your injured wrist?" I asked. "I can wait."

"I'll figure it out. You go."

"Don't forget to find out who Roxie is," I said. "And where she is."

"Roxie?"

"Yeah, remember the guy you cuffed back at the apartment? He told Eddie here to take Ana to Roxie's."

Rossi nodded. "We'll look into it. I'll be in touch." She waved us away, and Ana and I left in a hurry.

Once we were back in my SUV and before we hopped onto the interstate, I pulled over to a twenty-four-hour fast-food place with a drive-up window. We both ordered hamburgers and fries, a Coke for Ana, and another coffee for me.

As I drove up to the window, I gave Ana my phone. "Call your parents and tell them you're on your way back to Paterson. We should be there in three hours."

After she spoke to them—both ends of the conversation filled with tears and rapid explanations—Tomás asked to speak to me.

"My parents want you to know that they are very grateful that you have saved my sister. Thank you. We can hardly wait to see her."

"First, you're very welcome. Second, this was a team effort, and I'll pass along your appreciation. You'll see her very soon!" We signed off. Ana was smiling as she unwrapped her burger and started to eat.

I put on some music, a 1969 classic, "In the Year 2525" by Zager and Evens. The lyrics were perfect for my frame of mind after the last 24 hours.

CHAPTER TWENTY-THREE

It was a glorious, sunny morning by the time I exited the highway into Paterson. Ana was fast asleep with her seat as far back as it would go. It didn't take long to drive to the church where the undocumented workers had been transported after the warehouse. I was struck by how plain the brick structure was, built in another century with little decorative adornment. Still, the building felt sturdy, shielding the unique group sheltered there. It wasn't exactly a welcoming façade, but it meant freedom for this group that had been rescued from trafficking.

I pulled into the church's parking lot and gently nudged my passenger awake. "We're here, Ana."

She sleepily rubbed her eyes, stretched, and then bolted upright, as if she just remembered the night before and wondered where she was now. She looked around nervously and then at me, and her furrowed brow relaxed.

"Come on," I said. "Let's go find your family."

We walked over to the front of the church, up the

steps, and through the heavy doors. From the austerity and somberness of the outside of the building, we strode into the light streaming through stained glass windows that brightened up the nave where the congregation worshipped. This was a weekday, so it was almost completely empty.

Several voices called out to Ana in welcome. It was the Braga family. I watched her parents and brother make their way out of one of the pews and hurry over to her. I glanced at her in time to see a smile spread across her face.

Beatriz's eyes were overflowing with tears as she enveloped her daughter in a long embrace. Ana happily welcomed the hug as her father and brother piled on. All four members of the family sat together in a pew near the back, listening to Ana share the details of what had happened to her since the day before.

Even though I couldn't understand a word they were saying, it was the right moment to give them some privacy. I moved through one of the rows of pews to the other side of the church and quietly made my way in the shadows of the pillars that separated the aisle from the nave.

Marissa sat in a pew off to the side where the choir usually sang its hymns. She spoke with a man and a woman, and it appeared they were in deep conversation. Wedged between her and Natalia was the navy-blue messenger bag. Sam sat on Natalia's other side, her arm protectively around the ten-year-old. I watched the girl almost tip into Sam's lap and immediately fall asleep. Sam gently stroked her hair and looked up at me. She smiled, and I smiled back.

"They've got things really well-organized," Will said behind me. I startled slightly at the unexpected but quiet sound of his voice. "Glad you're back in one piece."

"Thanks." I nodded toward Marissa. "Are they from the U.S. Attorney's office? The two people she's talking to?"

"Yeah," he answered. "They've got a lot to discuss, but I think it's going very well."

Marissa pulled the navy bag out, dug around inside, and showed them the thumb drive. She put it back in the bag and pulled out a sheaf of papers and then put that back, too. She partially pulled out several pages and appeared to be giving the two attorneys quick explanations of what they were. Marissa tucked everything back in the messenger bag and handed it to them.

Meanwhile, the Braga family got up in the back, walked toward the altar, and made the sign of the cross as they left the nave through a door nearby.

"Where are they going?" I asked.

"They're taking Ana to the kitchen for a good, hot breakfast and then heading to their assigned cots in the fellowship hall, where I'd guess they'll try to sleep," Will said. "That's where everybody else is and they're exhausted. It was a stressful night for all of them."

"I'm sure many of them worried they'd be separated

permanently from other family members or friends," I said. "They're safe now, but do you think they believe it? Can they even fall asleep, or are they worried this could all change with the snap of their fingers?"

Will shook his head. "I'm sure none of us knows what it feels like to walk in their shoes."

"I agree. What's next for the group?"

"After they get some sleep, they'll first have assistance getting all the paperwork started. That way, they'll have the confidence of knowing that they can stay here and not get deported." Will stretched, extending his arms overhead. It had been a long night for everyone. "The other non-profits will step in and immediately organize housing. They'll try to keep the members of the group in close proximity to each other. Also, spending money and food vouchers are in order. And over the next few days, they'll get access to health care, a dental clinic, job training, and so on."

I looked over at Marissa, still talking with the two people from the U.S. Attorney's office. "And this is all happening because she's traded incriminating information on her father for their safety. Amazing."

"The feds have been after Maxim Popov for quite a while."

~~~~~

It was going on 9 am by the time I turned onto the gravel road leading to my house. I'd called my sister-in-law ahead, and Juliana had brought Warrior home. As I pulled up to the front door, I could hear him barking. It wasn't a guard-dog kind of bark, but a "happy you're home" bark.

The minute I opened the door, Warrior was almost in my arms. I dropped to my knees and embraced him. I could feel some of the tension of the last twenty-four hours release from my stiff neck as my face melted into his soft coat.

I poured a glass of smooth California Cabernet, went upstairs, and turned on the music. Willie Nelson's "Someone to Watch Over Me" from his hit Stardust album in the 1970s was perfect. I walked into my favorite room and turned on the faucet of the tub that sits like an island in the middle of the bathroom. I placed the wine glass by the tub and stripped off my clothes, dropping them onto the tile floor. Dipping my toe into the rapidly filling bath, I sighed at the warmth of the water. I stepped in and lowered myself into the tub.

"Oh, this is heaven." I sipped my wine and put my head back. My neck ached from the fight with Eddie, and the soak in the tub was just what I needed.

Warrior trotted over for a head scratch and then curled up, never taking his eyes off me. "You are such a good boy."

I looked up at the black-and-white photograph of Sean Connery, the famous one of him as James Bond in black tie, holding a gun. He was always my favorite spy, the one I liked to talk to during bath time when I have things on my mind.

"James, we came up against some really bad people in this trafficking case. I knew there was a lot of it out there, but I don't think it truly hit home for me until this case." I lowered my head. "I don't mean to sound naïve, but let's face it. Will and Sofia have been fighting crime a lot longer than I have. They're tougher than I am."

I took another sip of my wine. "I know. Stop whining. The last twenty-four hours are a reminder how I live in a privileged bubble. When I see firsthand these families being separated, and their hardship..." I skimmed the water with my fingers. "I don't know, James..."

I put down my glass, took a deep breath, and slid down, letting the bath water completely cover me.

CHAPTER TWENTY-FOUR

Several days later, I checked in with Will for an update. The U.S. Attorney's office had the process up and running for Maxim Popov's victims to become documented in the United States. Things were also moving smoothly with the organizations helping the group settle into their new lives. Marissa Popov and Samantha James were volunteers with one of the non-profits assisting the workers with services. Maxim Popov was now in custody. He'd been picked up trying to reenter the country in his private jet. His stateside financial accounts had also been frozen.

"How's Rossi doing?" I asked. "Will she still be able to shoot when the cast comes off?"

"She'll be fine," Will answered. "It'll take some time while her wrist heals, but it won't be long before she's back at the range."

"In the meantime, what can I do for her?" I asked. "I almost hate to admit it, but we were an effective team."

"Agreed." He paused. "She's taking a few days she

had coming to her, and right now, she's grousing around her place, but I have an idea."

~~~~~

I veered off the highway at one of the exits for Paterson. Warrior, strapped in on the passenger side of my SUV, gave a little yelp as he woke up and came to attention. It was as if my German shepherd knew this was the start of a novel adventure, and he was game.

Five minutes later, I drove through a community in transition. There was new construction taking place, and residents and owners were cleaning up the neighborhood. I approached a large old manufacturing building, admiring the brickwork of the four-story complex. This one had been transformed into apartments around two large courtyards that took up an entire double-sized block of real estate. This was the kind of building my daughters and their friends craved for apartment-living in Manhattan.

I parked in a guest slot inside one of the courtyards and clipped on Warrior's leash. Once he hopped out of the car, I grabbed a backpack with food and two large bags with supplies.

We slipped inside the building as a tenant exited. I checked the directory for names and we took the elevator to the fourth floor.

Warrior and I stood in front of the door. I pressed the buzzer and then a moment later knocked, too.

"Okay, okay," someone inside yelled. "Hold it, I'll be there in a second."

What a grumpy tone, I thought. I looked at my phone. Noon. I could see the door peephole darken for a moment.

"What are *you* doing here?"

I stared at the peephole. *You've got to be kidding, she's not going to open the door.*

The door swung open. Detective Sofia Rossi stood there with her left wrist in a cast that covered most of her lower arm. Her cool choppy haircut was a bed-head mess, and frankly looked great, along with her outfit of black leggings, sneakers, a grey oversized sweatshirt that said, "I'm only talking to my dog today."

"Do you have a dog?" was the first thing out of my mouth. I didn't remember her as being particularly dog friendly on a past case that involved a little terrier.

"I'm thinking about getting one." Rossi looked at my bags. "To what do I owe the honor of this uninvited visit, Lake?" She stared down at Warrior, whose tail wagged enthusiastically.

"May I come in?" I asked.

"As long as he doesn't tear around my place and scratch up the floor." She raised her eyebrows, which asked the question.

"Not a problem." *When do we get to the part where I feel welcome here*, I wondered. *Maybe her wrist hurts, and she's feeling crummy. Maybe this wasn't the right time to drop in.*

Rossi moved aside and opened the door wider for Warrior and me to enter. I stepped into a wonderful open loft space. It looked recently renovated, and a lot of light streamed in through tall new windows and reflected off highly varnished floors.

"What a great apartment!" I looked up at the ceiling, maybe twelve feet high.

"Thanks." Rossi's eyes were again on my dog.

I instructed Warrior to "wait" while I put down my bags. I pulled a small, round leopard-patterned cat bed out of one of the bags and put it on the floor. With only my hand signal, Warrior curled up into a tight knot to fit on the tiny bed, his favorite when we "travelled." His big brown eyes watched Rossi and me.

I pointed at her wrist. "Did you need a surgery?"

"No, I got lucky." She looked at her cast. "But I'll have this for the next couple of months."

"When we were driving down to Philadelphia, you mentioned you were planning to paint your apartment this weekend."

"Yeah," Rossi answered. "So?"

"And you were asking me for ideas about paint colors."

"I was making small-talk," she said. "But that project has been postponed, as you know." She held up her left arm, the one in the cast, and grimaced. Then her nose twitched. "Something smells good."

"I brought some take-out from the Aleppo Café—"

Immediately, her face lit up.

"Amazing food, right?" I walked toward the open kitchen with my backpack to get organized. "You sit still. I'll unpack it. Where are the dishes?"

She pointed toward a cabinet with her good arm, and I reached for two plates. "You're going to love this," I said, pulling two wraps out of the bag. "Have you had their shish tawook?"

"Yep."

"Don't you love that special sauce that they use on these?"

Rossi nodded, and I thought I saw a slight grin on her face. My dog picked up his head to catch the aroma, too, and looked at me with a mini-slurp.

"No, Warrior. This is not for you." I turned back to Rossi. "I even watched them use their special blender to whip up the sauce."

I walked over to her with our chicken wraps, bags of chips, and bottled iced tea. Rossi had sunk into one of four huge white round pouff seats. I sat on another of the pouffs and was surprised at how comfortable it was. We both grinned as we peeled back the paper around the wraps and opened our iced teas.

We sat quietly—we were too busy eating to talk much—while we enjoyed our food. The tender, juicy chicken marinated with yogurt, garlic, lemon, salt, and other spices was a home run.

"What's in those other bags?" She took another sip of iced tea and reached into her bag of chips for the last ones. The look in her eyes had shifted from friendly to suspicious.

"It's a surprise." I pulled out a sample paint card to

hand to her. "What do you think of Ledgetown Grey?"

"Not bad, but I'm kinda into white, in case you hadn't noticed." She gestured to the other white pouff chairs around her. I took our plates to the kitchen sink.

"And these chairs will really pop if you've got a subtle contrast on your walls." I rinsed the plates.

"Will really pop?" She looked amused and puzzled at the same time. "I'm not exactly the decorator type, you know. And as I said already, I'm into white."

"Yes, I heard you, but take that paint card and hold it against your chair." I put the dishes into the dishwasher. "Look at that pale grey against the white."

She did.

"What do you think? Pretty good, huh?"

"Okay, okay, I see your point—"

"The trim around the windows and the baseboards is already painted just about the same white as your chairs. Imagine if the walls were painted this color."

"Okay, I get it. You don't need to sell me on it. I like it," she said. "Hey, why are you so hot on *this* paint color."

I was already walking over to the two bags. "I used it at my house and it works like white. You still get a feeling of an open white space. It's a good thing you like it." I reached into the bags and pulled out two gallons of paint. "Look what I brought to get us going." I also laid out other supplies for the job—two paint trays, different sized rollers and brushes, an extension pole, painter's tape, an angled brush for corners, and a paint stick for mixing. "You got a ladder?"

"Yes, but wait a minute—"

"I knew you'd wanted to start painting, but you've got that bum wrist for the time being." I marched over to Rossi with the cans of Ledgetown Grey paint. "So I'm here to work...you know, to help you get settled in this fantastic apartment." I put the cans down and marched back for brushes, paint trays, and a tarp.

"Hold on, Lake." She used her uninjured arm to push herself up from the big chair. "You can't just come in her and take over—"

"I'm not taking over," I protested. "I'm trying to say thank you for helping me save Ana. That was some kind of move, jumping off that truck and landing right on top of Eddie. I've never seen anything like it before."

"It's my job."

"I know it's your job, but that doesn't matter. It was still amazing. Helping you paint is my way of saying thank you," I said. "Anyway, you like the color. I could at least paint a sample, and you could see for yourself and decide. And if you don't like it, that's fine. I'll take the cans home." I waited.

And waited as she looked at the paint chip against her white chair. And waited some more as she finished her iced tea.

Finally, Rossi turned toward me. "I'm used to doing everything for myself." Another long pause.

She stared at her cast. "Okay, you're on. I accept your offer." She sighed. "It's a very nice thing that you're doing. Thank you." Her eyes met mine and then moved to the paint cans. "But only if you let me pay for these supplies. I don't want any free hand-outs."

CHAPTER TWENTY-FIVE

The walls were already white—albeit a boring white—and in good shape, so we didn't need any primer. I spread out a tarp to protect the beautiful floor. After painting a good-sized sample of grey on one of the walls, Rossi approved the color.

I climbed up high on her ladder. Using the cutting brush, I painted a clean edge at the top of the wall where it met the ceiling. "How'd you find this very cool apartment anyway?"

"I walked by this building a lot. Once the construction started, a sign went up about future apartments. I got on the waiting list right away." Rossi organized some of the paint supplies and then leaned against the island counter, watching me paint.

"What was it like growing up in Paterson?" I kept my brush moving very carefully to get that razor-sharp edge. I dipped into a tray for more paint.

She rolled her eyes. "Lake, it was just like growing up anywhere else."

"Were you born in Paterson?" I climbed down the

ladder, moved it over, and caught her eye roll. Maybe she thought I was being too nosy. I climbed right back up to repeat the edging on a fresh section of the wall. "Full disclosure, I was born at Morristown Hospital."

"And I was born at St. Joe's Hospital." She chuckled. "Even though they take everyone, you know what they say about St. Joe's? That every Catholic in Paterson was born there." She laughed at her own joke. Hearing Rossi laughing was a new experience for me. I chuckled, too.

"Where I grew up, I can't say that every Episcopalian was born at Morristown Hospital. There were probably a lot of them, and a lot of Catholics, too, and everybody else."

I was back down on the floor painting a clean edge above the baseboard. This required total focus, so there was a conversational pause on both our parts. The quiet was nice. Could it be that Rossi and I were actually getting comfortable enough with each other that we could enjoy the silence?

I used an extension pole with one of the rollers and filled in the top half of the wall where I'd completed the edge. I could hear Rossi moving around behind me.

Music faded up in the apartment, not too loud, and the sorrowful saxophone immediately identified the huge hit of a famous Nigerian-born singer. I turned around. "Sofia! You're a fan of Sade, too," I exclaimed. "I love 'The Sweetest Taboo.'"

Rossi closed her eyes and slightly nodded. "I love

all her music." She picked up a roller. "Okay, I think I'm ready to give this a try. I'm a lefty, but if I go slow, I think I can manage the roller with my right."

I set her up where I'd completed the top half of the wall. She pulled over a short stepladder, sat down, and began very slowly working on the bottom half.

We both enjoyed the quiet with Sade in the background. I repeated the entire process of carefully painting the edges to the ceiling and down below to the baseboard and then the top half of the wall for another ten feet. As I moved down the wall, Rossi followed slowly behind on the lower part of the wall, getting better at using the roller with her right hand.

Four songs and twenty minutes later. "Hey Sofia, where did you live when you were a kid? Was it nearby?" I dipped my brush in the tray, careful not to carry too much paint to the wall.

She shook her head. "Now you want to know my history?" She didn't know me well enough to understand that I'm just naturally curious about people.

"Just interested, that's all," I said.

"I grew up at the corner of East 38th Street and 18th Avenue, and no, it's not close to here. It's over in the Eastside section," she said patiently, but she was starting to sound a little testy. "Which is not like the east side in Manhattan. In Paterson, the bigger houses are off Eastside Park. Where I lived, well, it was solidly middle class. So, I went to PS20 and then to Eastside High. What about you?"

"I wasn't in a city, or even near a city. My experience was more rural," I answered. "A lot of developers have come out to where I live, and the open countryside has gotten a lot smaller since I was a kid."

Rossi walked over to the kitchen, turned on a faucet and filled a glass of water. She held it up to me.

"No thanks. I'm good." I was back on the ladder, and I stretched to paint the last section I could reach.

Rossi chugged most of the water in the glass.

I moved the ladder further down, poured more paint into the tray, and climbed back up. "Where do you go to college when you want to be a cop?"

"John Jay College of Criminal Justice." She gave me a look like I didn't know anything. It was one that was familiar to me when working with her.

"That's in the city, isn't it?"

"Yep." She stared at the section she was painting. "I always wanted to live in Manhattan for a while, so that's where I went to school."

"Is John Jay like going to Harvard if you want to be a cop?"

"Yep."

Rossi finished another section, and she stood up and stretched. "Where did you go and what did you study?"

"History," I answered, "at Penn."

"Be right back." She headed down a hall to the back of the apartment.

I continued painting and then moved the ladder again to finish the high end of that wall.

When Rossi returned, she was definitely moving more slowly than usual.

"Please, take a break, Sofia, if you're in pain or just plain old tired." I wanted to encourage her to slow down. I was hoping she wouldn't take my head off at the suggestion. She surprised me.

"Okay, but just for five minutes." Rossi plopped down on her pouff chair and sank right into it. Warrior walked over and curled up next to her big white pouff. She looked down at him and tentatively scratched his head. "I'm on pain killers for my wrist. Do *not* let me fall asleep," she ordered.

She did anyway, and while she slept and Warrior snored quietly, I continued painting the last bottom-half section of the wall. My phone pinged and I found a text from Sam.

-*Good news. I got the part.*

-On the series about the law firm?

-*Yeah. I'm the rebellious law student who interns there.*

-Congrats! Sounds like typecasting. LOL. When do you start?

-*Right after Thanksgiving.*

-You're going to be one busy lady with the TV show and your volunteer work with Marissa.

-Yeah. I like it that way.

-Will you be with Marissa and Natalia for Thanksgiving?

-Yep, the 3 of us. We're gonna to cook a bird.

-Why don't you come out to my place and join my family for Thanksgiving?

-As long as you don't do your mom-thing. LOL just kidding. Thank you. Will check with Marissa.

-Great. Let me know. And congrats on landing the part!

I picked up the roller and resumed painting.

Rossi awoke with a start as I finished painting the bottom corner. Done. I stood back to admire the color. "It looks pretty good, if I do say so myself."

She rubbed her eyes and gazed at the wall. "The color does look good," she agreed, plain and simple.

Now that we were finished with the first wall, we stared at the really long one that went the entire length of the apartment, grinned at the same moment, burst out laughing, and decided to work on another smaller wall. We would also decide once the paint was dry on the finished wall whether it even needed another coat.

We approached the second wall the way we painted

the first one and developed a nice rhythm as the afternoon wore on. Our conversation got easier, and we learned more about each other. I told her about my work in cable TV distribution, my kids, my son's death in Afghanistan, and my divorce. She told me how she had started with the Teaneck Police Department and then moved up the ladder when she worked at the Hackensack PD and became a detective. Then she moved to a smaller department out my way for personal reasons. She did not explain if the personal reasons included a relationship, and there was no way I'd touch that question with a ten-foot pole. The most I dared explore were the pros and cons of large versus small police departments and if she missed the larger ones where she'd worked. She did not.

As I opened a bag of freshly baked cookies and put them on a plate, I also learned that her family had been in Paterson for a long time. Her forebears had come from the Italian silk city, Como, in the early twentieth century. Her great-grandfather had worked his way up in a silk factory in Paterson and would become one of many to own a small family mill with only a few looms.

"They were called 'cockroach' shops," Rossi said. "It sounds creepy, but it's not."

"How did that work? These cockroach shops?" I asked, holding out the plate of cookies.

"You'd have a large, old, multi-story mill building and subdivide it into smaller sections for these family mills. It was a way for the weavers to become modest capitalists." She put down her roller and chose two cookies. "Maybe my great-grandfather had dreams of becoming another William Strange."

I gave her a blank stare. "Who?"

"He was a city father when my great-grandfather came here from Italy."

"Of course," I said. "William Strange. So, he was a big deal in Paterson?" I helped myself to a couple of cookies, too.

"One of the leading silk industrialists in the entire country," Sofia said. "Definitely a city father back in the day." She applied more paint to her roller and continued with the lower wall. "Anyway, my great-grandfather Rossi wanted to make a better life for his family. His son, my grandfather, was the same way, and he pounded it into us at the dinner table that education was the path."

"It sounds like they were both hard-working and had an entrepreneurial spirit," I said, munching on a lemon cookie.

"I adored my grandpops," she said. "Most of his kids got a college degree, some on the G.I. Bill. And I think all my cousins, we all went to college." She took a chocolate chip cookie with her free hand, bit into it, and an expression of bliss passed over her face as she ate it.

"Your family's definitely the all-American success story," I added. "We're all immigrants at some point or another, aren't we? My family came from England on my father's side, and from Germany on my mother's side. Are you Italian on both sides?"

"Yeah."

We kept painting the wall with our rollers. Along the way, we examined the first wall, which was dry, and decided another coat of paint was unnecessary.

"This color looks great," Rossi said.

I agreed. It really suited the apartment. We finished up the second wall, enjoying the music and lost in our thoughts.

A little later, we decided to go for it and attack the very long wall. We continued our quiet companionship and pushed ahead.

It was getting to be late afternoon and we were halfway down that wall. I was surprised at how well Rossi managed painting with her non-broken right wrist. She got better and faster as the day progressed.

Finally, she stopped to pull two bottles out of the refrigerator. "How about a beer?"

"Sure." I was ready for a short break.

Rossi pulled an opener out of a drawer as I came down the ladder. She struggled to open the bottles with her non-dominant right hand, and it wasn't happening. She looked at me sheepishly. "I guess I could crack it against the countertop, but that might be—"

"Give it here, Sofia."

She reluctantly handed me the opener. "I'm somewhat limited by this bum wrist." She moved it slightly, wiggling her fingers at the end of the cast.

I opened both beers and filled Warrior's travel water

bowl. As my German shepherd slurped, we clinked the bottles, drank a little, and continued painting.

It didn't feel like we'd run out of conversation. More like we were focused on finishing. Thoughts of Yolanda snuck in and upset my concentration. I was chewing on my lip again and nervously tapping my foot on one step of the ladder.

Rossi glanced up at the sound. "You okay?"

"I don't know…"

"Come on," she urged. "Spill it."

"I can't stop thinking about Yolanda Hernandez… that she's the only one missing in that entire group of—what was the final head count?"

"Forty-seven plus the four from the nail salon," she answered. "Remember, she's not the only one. Mrs. Cara and her two kids are also missing. None of them were there when the police arrived. I'm betting the boss ran with the kids and forced the nanny to come with them."

"She may not have had to force the nanny," I said. "According to Yolanda, Mrs. Cara was a terrible mother, and not their real mother."

"Not their real mother?"

"That's why Yolanda wouldn't leave with me when I went back to the house to pick her up. She was devoted to those girls."

"It sounds like she's a good person." Rossi got back to it with the roller, painting the very last section of this third wall.

I'd finished and started cleaning up. But I couldn't let it go. "I keep wondering if there was something else I could have done for Yolanda. I feel like I failed her."

"You did all you could do—"

"Don't think I'm crazy, Sofia, but I think I need to look for her, to try to find her."

"Lake, listen here. You'll do no such thing," she said to me, back in detective-mode with a toughness in her voice. "People disappear inside the borders of our country all the time. How are you supposed to find an undocumented person in the middle of three-hundred-thirty-million people? Yolanda will disappear, if she hasn't already."

"Why doesn't she call her cousin Manuel? He's safe with the others. Or me? I gave her my phone number." I remembered how she had me write it with a pen on the side of her midriff under her tee-shirt so the boss wouldn't see it. "Hey, Sofia." I pointed at the brushes with a questioning look.

"It's latex paint. Use the sink."

I turned the water on to rinse the brushes. "It doesn't make sense that she doesn't call anyone."

"Maybe she doesn't have her phone. Who knows? And if she does, would you call if you were hiding in this country illegally?"

"No, but—"

"No buts, Ronnie. All you can do is hope they're okay."

"I get it, Sofia, but this is really eating at me, the way these victims just disappear. You know, that could have happened to Ana and the two sisters if we hadn't gotten to them in time."

"But we did get there in time," Rossi snapped. "Look, everybody's after that Mrs. Cara, and that means they'll find Yolanda and the girls, too. You have to trust that she's okay. This isn't over."

"If you say so."

Warrior picked up on the disheartening tone in my voice and came over to nuzzle against my leg. I sat on the floor and he put his head on my shoulder. I gave him an enormous hug, rubbing his deep, smooth coat. He made quiet but reassuring noises. Then he pulled back and stared at me with his soulful brown eyes.

"Warrior, you know just when I need a hug. You are such a good boy."

I got up to finish putting everything away. "Sofia, I'm going to leave these supplies with you, in case you want to extend this color down that hallway."

"Thank you, Ronnie. Good suggestion. I'll think about it."

"And I'm available to come back and help you finish," I said. "If you'd like."

Rossi stood there as if she was considering the offer, but she didn't jump at it. Instead, she leaned over and rubbed the top of Warrior's head.

"Hey, I need to take him for a quick walk before we leave—"

"I've got an idea. We'll walk him over to the old Little Italy, to Ciancy Street. We need a proper coffee after that delicious lunch and all our hard work. Plus, there's a nice little bakery over there we can visit."

"What do you mean the *old* Little Italy?" I asked as I clipped Warrior's leash to his collar.

"Well, one of Paterson's immigrant neighborhoods was called Dublin, and then it became Little Italy, and now it's mostly Little Lima," she said, "but Ciancy Street still has some Italian clubs and cafés and this bakery."

"How far is it from you, because I really have to get going." I looked at the time on my phone, and packed Warrior's nest in one of the bags.

Rossi took that bag as I picked up my pack. "It's not far, just over by the Great Falls. You and Warrior are gonna love it." She opened the door. "Come on. Let's put these things in your car."

Down on the street, I locked the car and asked, "Which way?"

"Follow me," she answered. Warrior and I followed.

"Did you know," Detective Sofia Rossi said as we walked in the direction of the Falls, "that Paterson has around 146,000 residents?"

"Oh, boy, now I'm in for the fifty-cent tour—" My darling dog barked in agreement.

That didn't stop Rossi, her voice crystal-clear, even as Warrior and I lagged behind slightly. "...And, did you know, Private Investigator Ronnie Lake, that there are fifty-two ethnic populations in this city which means there are loads of different restaurants, clubs, bakeries, cafés and take-out..."

I put my finger to my mouth to signal quiet as Warrior and I stopped for a moment to see if Rossi would notice, but she didn't as she continued her Paterson tour happily strolling down the street. She was completely immersed in the history of her hometown as she headed toward the Great Falls and her voice grew more distant. I thought I heard her say "Alexander Hamilton" and the "Industrial Revolution."

Warrior and I hurried to catch up.

Epilogue

It was hard to believe that I could be driving in my bright red Mustang with the top down and Warrior next to me on Thanksgiving. Besides this beautiful New Jersey day, I had a lot to be thankful for.

I was thrilled for the rescued trafficking victims, of course. As I headed off to spend today with some of the most special people in my life, I wondered how those courageous people would celebrate their fresh start in this country.

The only shadow for me was that Yolanda Hernandez was still missing from the group. I took a deep inhale of fresh air.

Usually, it was pretty chilly at this time of year, but I could feel the warmth of sunshine on my face. Even with the low-sixties temperature, I had still layered up, just in case. I always felt carefree while riding along these twisty back-country roads. Warrior and I loved it, and I turned up the music.

> *...And we'll walk in the sun*
> *But til then tramps like us*
> *Baby, we were born to run...*

That we were also listening to Bruce Springsteen's "Born to Run" made it really great. The perfect song for these roads.

I turned left at Meadow Farm and continued driving on the long dirt road that meandered through alternating woods and fields and fenced-in pastures for the Meadow Farm sheep. I came around a bend, and Warrior voiced his happy bark as the beautiful stone and stucco house with a slate roof came into view. Beautiful to me, of course, because it always reminded me of a wonderful childhood growing up here decades ago.

Warrior loved coming here, too, lately because he had a new little four-legged friend who'd become part of my big brother's household. Frank and Joan Rutherfurd had raised their children here until his beloved wife died two-and-a-half years ago. After some time as a widower, he met the wonderful Juliana and had remarried.

Once parked, Warrior and I stepped into the house's elegant two-story octagonal foyer. "Hellooo," I called. "Anybody home?"

I could hear a lot of talking and laughing coming from the kitchen. Before I set off in that direction, Frank and Juliana came down the grand stairway that curved along the eight-sided wall as it descended to the first floor.

"Hi, Sis," my six-foot-two brother called out. "Jules and I are happy to see you."

"Oh, Ronnie!" His wife's astoundingly gorgeous features—the high cheekbones, the cat-like eyes, the full lips—broke into an enormous smile. "All the kids—yours, his, I think mine is still upstairs—anyway they're all in the kitchen. I'm not sure what's going on in there, but they've promised the perfect feast and won't let us do anything."

As soon as my German shepherd heard Juliana's voice, his tail had started swishing back and forth. I instructed Warrior to wait, and he sat obediently as Juliana and Frank and I embraced, full of Thanksgiving greetings. My brother's handsome, weather-beaten face grinned at me, and I affectionately messed his salt-and-pepper hair, an old habit from childhood.

Juliana walked to the stairway and sat down on the third step. Warrior's tail picked up more and more speed like a car windshield wiper on its fastest setting. My sister-in-law looked at me and I nodded. She tapped the step and my dog trotted over. He sat right in front of her and looked at her adoringly. She rubbed Warrior's head and leaned over to speak quietly into his ear.

My big, tough German shepherd made a hilarious-sounding squeal and rolled over on his back awaiting a tummy rub. Juliana quickly obliged him.

"Sis, tell me about Marissa, Natalia, and Sam, our special guests today."

"They rented a car in the city." I looked at my phone. "They should be here any minute."

"So, how'd you meet them and how in the world did you ever get involved in a human trafficking case?" Frank asked.

"Well, first I met Sam, uh, you might say accidentally. Her name's Samantha James."

"What do you mean by 'accidentally?'" my brother asked.

"To be honest, it really started before that when I found the Louis Vuitton duffle in the taxi."

Juliana continued focusing on Warrior, but piped up, "Samantha lost a Vuitton duffle in a taxi?"

"No, someone else did. I wanted to track down the owner and the cab driver got nastier and nastier. He'd say things like 'my cab, my bag' and I knew he'd never turn it in to lost and found."

"What does that have to do with Samantha James?" my brother asked.

"A lot, because he tried to grab it, so I jumped out of the cab with the duffle. And then the driver jumped out of the cab in the middle of all the traffic and almost came after me to take it."

"What did you do, Ronnie, to stay away from this crazy man?" Juliana asked, burying her chin in Warrior's coat.

"I hid in an office building, while all the cars were honking at this guy to move his taxi. And he finally did and drove off." I paused a moment remembering how relieved I'd felt when he left the scene and I still had the bag.

"And?" Frank prompted. "Get to the Samantha part."

"I came out of the building with all my bags and stepped right in the way of Samantha James, who's a part-time bike messenger. She missed me, but crashed on her bike."

"Are you going to tell me she jumped up and told you she needed to hire a private eye?"

I looked at my big brother as if he was impossible, just like when we were kids, but I could see he had a slight smile playing around the corners of his mouth. "Frank. Cut it out."

"Was Samantha okay after her crash?" Juliana asked.

"Thank you, Juliana. Yes, she did not have any injuries except a scraped leg and forearm where she landed. But I felt so guilty and wanted to help."

"Oh, no," my brother moaned. "Here it comes."

"Frank," my sister-in-law mock-scolded.

I continued with my saga. "Anyway, she received a text that got her all upset. And I offered to help, but she was kind of mad at me for the bike crash, of course, and did not want my help."

Frank rolled his eyes, and Juliana giggled into Warrior's coat.

"Do you want to hear the rest or not?" I felt a bit disgruntled that they didn't seem to be taking me seriously. "I'm getting to the good part."

"Yes, yes, we do, Ronnie." Juliana nodded her head, her tone full of kindness and sincerity, unlike my big brother.

"I pulled out my business card and handed it to her in case she changed her mind, and she rode away." I stopped for dramatic effect.

They both looked at me waiting.

"You have a business card?" my brother asked.

I nodded.

"What does it say? Nosy Private Eye ready to solve your case?" He was enjoying chuckling at his own jokes, which was nothing new. "Maybe with a Charlie's Angels kind of silhouette logo?"

"This is why I don't tell you much about my work, Frank. My card says Veronica Rutherfurd Lake, Private Investigator, with my cell phone, email and New Jersey PI License number. A plain white card with black text, thank you." I paused, a very pregnant pause, staring at Frank. "And a half hour later, guess who texted me for help."

"Samantha James," they said in unison.

"And that's how I landed in the middle of a kidnapping case that turned into a trafficking case—"

"Okay, okay, I get it," Frank said. "There's more to this story—"

"But what happened to the Luis Vuitton duffle?" Juliana interrupted.

"That was a mini-investigation with a happy ending, too."

Frank rolled his eyes.

"Stop, Frank," Juliana said in her most endearing voice. "I want to know."

"Okay, how about the short version?" he asked.

"There was an orange Hermès scarf box in the duffle. I took it to the Hermès store and lovely Chloe there helped me track down the couple who owned the bag. I met them in Manhattan early this week and they were so happy to have it back that they wanted to give me a reward, which I turned down, of course."

"You turned down the reward? Really?" Frank asked.

"Really. But I haven't told you the best part. We got to talking about the case in Paterson, and they put me in touch with their son, who, guess what, is an immigration lawyer. He's now helping several of the more complicated cases in the Paterson group."

Juliana jumped in. "That's amazing—"

A voice from upstairs yelled, "They're here. They're here!!!" I could hear footfalls hurrying down the hallway.

All of us looked up as a slender, dark-haired young teenaged girl arrived at the top of the stairs. Juliana's daughter radiated excitement as she clung to a wiggly, white fur-ball. Francesca instructed the tiny dog in her arms with her most grown-up voice as she walked down the steps, "Now Lucy, stop wiggling so much."

"Aha, Lucy's been hiding with you upstairs, Frankie," my brother said. "I've been looking all over for her."

Warrior was squirming with excitement at the prospect of being with his tiny friend. Francesca leaned over so the two dogs could give each other face licks and kisses. Then she marched straight to the window with Lucy still in her arms, and all of us, including

Warrior, followed to look outside.

A metallic green Subaru Outback drove on the gravel road to the house.

"The people in the car are special, and that's why they are having Thanksgiving with us?" Francesca asked me.

"They are very special. Samantha—you'll see she has the red hair—and Marissa—she has the blonde hair—did something very brave."

"How were they brave, Aunt Ronnie?"

"They helped save a group of about fifty women and men from some very bad people, so they are special," I said. "And Marissa has a little sister, Natalia. I think she's ten."

"She's a little girl," Francesca noted.

"Yes, and you have an important job this Thanksgiving."

Francesca looked up at me, attentively waiting for her instructions. I signaled Warrior to wait and then continued.

"You are in charge of making Natalia feel very welcome among all these grown-ups, showing her around, and paying attention to her," I said. "Can you do it—"

Francesca was already out of the house before I could finish. We walked through the door as the car parked. She was already waving at one of the windows and opening the door.

"Hi, Natalia. I'm Frankie. Welcome to Meadow Farm."

Natalia stepped out of the back, while Marissa and Sam got out of the front.

Francesca continued. "This is our dog, Lucy." She reached the little dog out to Natalia. "Would you like to hold her? She's very friendly and cuddly."

Natalia looked up at Francesca as if she were the coolest girl in the neighborhood, maybe even cooler than her sister Marissa, at least for the moment.

A huge grin spread across her face. "Yes, please." She held out her arms and Francesca gently placed Lucy, who had calmed down, into Natalia's arms.

We stood by the door as Samantha, Marissa, Natalia, and Francesca all fussed over the little dog. Frank, Juliana, Warrior, and I walked over to welcome them.

~~~~~

Some hours later, we had all finished our Thanksgiving feast and were helping clean up in the kitchen. I asked to speak to Marissa privately.

We walked into the library and I gestured toward one of the upholstered chairs where she should sit down.

"Here. This is for you." I handed her a large brown envelope that I'd brought with me.

"Should I open it now?" Marisa asked.

"Wait until you get back to the city, then make yourself a cup of tea, sit down and read it." I was working my way to breaking the news to her gently, but

I knew it would be a painful blow no matter how she learned of it.

"What's this about?" she asked.

I took a seat and paused for a moment, then said, "I know this is going to be a terrible shock, but your stepmother may still be alive."

Marissa dropped the envelope to her lap. "What did you just say?" Her voice shook.

"Kate Popov may be alive," I repeated.

"I mean, how do you know?" She picked up the envelope and stared at it. "Where is she?"

I explained how my suspicions had been aroused during my conversation with the man in front of the factory. "Right after I dropped you at the church, I started looking into it. And most of what I found is in that envelope."

"The proof that she's alive?" She gestured with the envelope, her hand shaking.

"Look, I don't know anything for sure, and that's why I think you shouldn't tell Natalia yet. But I don't think her mother's dead," I answered. "I haven't been able to track down a death certificate in New Jersey or New York, only a missing person's report filed by her sister."

"I remember her sister. Why wouldn't she call me and tell me? For Natalia's sake." Her tone was angry.

"Maybe because she didn't want to get your hopes up? But I haven't had a chance to speak with her yet. I did track down a bank account and a safe deposit box here in New Jersey. I also found the deed to property over in Pennsylvania that Kate Popov owned."

Tears rolled down Marissa's cheeks. "If she got away, why wouldn't Mama Kate take us with her? Why would she leave us behind?"

"There's another document in the envelope that will shed light—"

"What's that?" she demanded, sounding even angrier.

"She had a restraining order against your father—"

"What?" she gasped.

"Maybe she was so scared of your dad or was concerned for your safety, and that's why she couldn't reach out to you. In the restraining order, she accused him of physical abuse and she was trying to leave him—"

"Where'd you get all of this information?" Marissa held up the envelope.

"I did a lot of research and made a lot of phone calls. I called in some favors with friends on the police force, that kind of thing. Look, I don't want to get your hopes up—"

Marissa Popov interrupted, now cool as a cucumber. "No, it's too late for that. I've always held onto this hope, you know? I'd already lost my mom, and losing my stepmother was almost as painful. Then, the way it happened—I wasn't allowed to go to the funeral so I could stay home and watch Natalia, we never got to go to the hospital after she supposedly had a car accident..."

Her voice trailed off for a moment and she had a

faraway look, clearly remembering so many things at once. It was like I could actually see on her face the puzzle pieces falling into place in her mind. Suddenly, she looked at me with the same kind of fierceness I'd seen when she offered to trade the evidence against her own father—evidence she'd been carefully tucking away in case it would ever prove useful—for the freedom of dozens of innocent strangers.

"Are you up for another case, Ronnie?"

The End

For more information on the plague of human trafficking, visit:

https://polarisproject.org/myths-facts-and-statistics/

https://www.dhs.gov/blue-campaign/indicators-human-trafficking

Want to know what happened to Yolanda?
Visit here for an extended epilogue!
https://dl.bookfunnel.com/o8krsutnpn

Sign up for Niki Danforth's newsletter to learn
about upcoming new releases —

https://nikidanforth.com/

ACKNOWLEDGEMENTS

It has been my good fortune to work with the same team on all of the Ronnie Lake books. Without the kindness, support, and expertise of the following people, *Traffic: A Ronnie Lake Mystery* would still be a work-in-progress:

Leonard A. Zax, president of the Hamilton Partnership for Paterson, New Jersey, and a born-and-bred Paterson native, guided me in the passages about his hometown;

Lt. Vito Abrusci (Retired), Mendham Township Police Department, New Jersey, is my go-to resource when it comes to his invaluable input on correct law enforcement procedures in the Ronnie Lake Series;

Karen De Paola, 6th Dan, SkylandsAikikai.com, consultant for Aikido and fight scenes in all the Ronnie Lake books, helps me keep it real;

Dr. Lisa M. Bonaventura, an internist in Bedminster, NJ, took time out from her busy practice to guide me on

Detective Sofia Rossi's broken wrist and Marissa Popov's bloody nose;

Walter Sutton, senior training manager for The Seeing Eye, Inc., continues to share his extensive knowledge of the German shepherd breed, so critical to writing the character of retired war dog Warrior, Ronnie's trusted four-legged companion;

My fantastic editor, Mercy Pilkington, challenges and pushes me in my growth as a writer, as well as working with me to deliver the best book I can;

Other wonderful colleagues, friends, and family were a source of support and inspiration along the way, especially Jane Balaguero and my marvelous husband Dan.

Words cannot fully express the gratitude I feel for their help and encouragement.

N.D. August 2021

AUTHOR'S NOTE:
A LITTLE SOMETHING ON PATERSON

When the gritty New Jersey city of Paterson, just fifteen miles west of Manhattan, became the main location for this Ronnie Lake novel, I dove into the research, as all authors do, to make sure my portrayal was accurate and true. Many people falsely assume Paterson has a bad reputation. I was fortunate to be able to turn for guidance to Leonard A. Zax, born and bred in Paterson and a true leader in its comeback story. He says it so well:

Like virtually every historic industrial city in America, deindustrialization hit Paterson very hard. But unlike virtually every old industrial city in America, Paterson never suffered to 30 or 40 or 50 percent decline in population that hit Newark and Camden, Detroit, and Cleveland, and so many other smaller industrial cities.

The population today is higher than it has ever been, powered by generations of new immigrants who add new vitality and spirit to the city. A hundred years ago the immigrants spoke Italian, Russian, Polish, and Yiddish. Today they speak Spanish, Arabic, Turkish, and Bengali. The languages are different today but the aspirations are the same: a better life for their families.

Paterson spiraled downward for decades but has turned the corner and today is on a trajectory of hope.

As I wrote this book, Leonard shared with me all sorts of articles and links. Here are some of my favorites.

This is a good overview of the city as it experiences its transformation:
https://www.nytimes.com/2018/07/05/nyregion/paterson-nj-revitalization.html

The centerpiece of the city is the Paterson Great Falls, the country's newest national historic park:
https://www.hamiltonpartnership.org/national-park/natural-wonder

Next to the Great Falls is Hinchliffe Stadium, which hosted many Negro Leagues baseball games starting back in the 1930s and is at the start of its own comeback story:
https://www.forbes.com/sites/danschlossberg/2021/04/05/historic-hinchliffe-stadium-where-larry-doby-started-due-for-facelift/?sh=2d2b55cb59ff

NEED MORE RONNIE LAKE IN YOUR LIFE?

FIND OUT ABOUT PREVIOUS TITLES IN THE RONNIE LAKE SERIES:

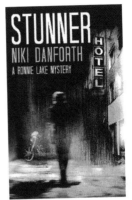

Beautiful. Bright. And possibly deadly…

This is all Ronnie Lake knows about her potential sister-in-law, Juliana. Who is this mysterious woman with two lives—and how deep does her deception go?

As a divorced, downsized, 50-something, Ronnie finds herself becoming an "accidental detective" in order to get to the bottom of things.

With her trusty German Shepherd by her side, Ronnie jumps into this action-packed adventure in the first novel in the *Ronnie Lake Series* about a crime of abduction and family betrayal.

Here's what readers are saying:

"It's nice to see a P. I. at the beginning of their journey."

"Fabulous suspenseful story…Niki Danforth is the new James Patterson!"

"A great book about one family's struggle to reconcile the past with the present."

Ronnie Lake's second chapter in life has just begun, but the sleuth-in-training didn't expect her first real investigation would lead to a 40-year-old crime. She vows to solve the cold case before her dying client takes his last breath.

Racing against the clock, she sets a dangerous trap that could lure her prime suspect into handcuffs...or trigger another bloody rampage.

This cold case is the second installment in the *Ronnie Lake Series*.

Here's what readers are saying:

"Loved the way Ronnie Lake put the pieces together."

"A cold case, clues only a woman might notice, look out killer here comes justice."

"The perfect airport read, in the tradition of Mary Higgins Clark!"

A rare edition. A murdered thief. Can a rookie P.I. solve the case before the killer ending?

After discovering that a rare edition of *The Great Gatsby* is at the center of a murder, Ronnie dives deep into the world of collecting. But when her investigation brings her closer to a rich book connoisseur with an eye for romance, she's unsure if he's a partner or a suspect. He's handsome, wealthy, and mysterious...but you can't judge a book by its cover, can you, in this suspenseful tale, the third book in the *Ronnie Lake Series*.

Here's what readers are saying:

"Niki Danforth has put together a gripping mystery with an appealing heroine."

"The author writes similar to my favorite author Janet Evanovich."

"Well written with well developed, relatable characters."

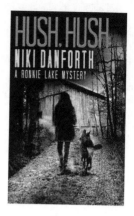

Private detective Ronnie Lake accepts a case tracking down a young runaway. Her search quickly points to a far more sinister crime.

Sniffing out clues with her loyal German Shepherd, the determined investigator uncovers a brutal crime and meddling authorities. The abduction leads to shadowy powerbrokers and political intrigue, putting her directly in the crosshairs in this fourth novel in the *Ronnie Lake Series*.

Here's what readers are saying:

"This book brought me back to all the hours spent with a Sue Grafton book, following the life and adventures of Kinsey Millhone."

"This is a solid whodunit…"

"Ronnie Lake is a great character. Smart, courageous, capable and driven to solve mysteries…will keep you turning pages fast."

"…a damn fine mystery and a well-crafted detective novel."